SKINWALKERS

THE UPRISING

PART TWO

A Novel by

Monica L. Smith

To submit a manuscript for our review,

email us at

submissions@majorkeypublishing.com

Dedication

I would like to dedicate this book to the ladies who gave me the idea of writing a book about Skinwalkers. Although I have changed a lot of it to suit the needs of this story, it was because of Rebecca, Ashley, Sharon, and Micah that I created this book.

I gain a lot of knowledge from each one of you and have even borrowed your names. From the deepest depths of my heart to its surface, I want to say thank you for all your support, your input, and your guidance.

Chapter One

Lana

Right after the funeral detail came to pick up my precious babies, I had made up my mind that I had to rid our home of that infectious disease, Ashley. Since Gethambe started messing around with her, he has changed, and not for the better. His top priority is her, not me, his children, the people, or our traditions…just Ashley. I hate her being with every drop of blood in my body. I wish she was dead.

I waited patiently for them to take my babies to the ceremonial room before going down to the hot springs for a bath. I had learned a long time ago that there were plenty of secret tunnels that lead throughout our establishment. And one in particular that led you to just outside of the compound to where I knew the mountain lions hung out regularly. I would be safe because I was going to make them an offer that they couldn't resist.

I slid my body between the small opening behind the waterfall portion of our hot spring bath. Funny how no one has ever found this one; it was so obvious. When I entered the dark tunnel, I transformed into my beast and began to run through the dimly lit tunnel. I followed it for about ten miles to where the Navajo reservation met up with Winslow. It took me quite some time to get there, but it was well worth it.

When I exited the tunnel, I shifted back into my human form and made my way to the Lion's Den restaurant. Yes, I was totally nude, but I was going into a place that was mostly filled with male, lower level mountain lions.

I opened the door and blew past the greeter and stood in the middle of their restaurant and said, "I'm looking for the one they call, GG. We have some business to discuss."

One of the mountain lions came up to me and sniffed into the air. Because there were a few human customers that were watching, he decided to back down and take his seat at his table. He knew who I was, and I knew what he was. Hell, I could hardly tolerate the heavy aroma of wet cats that filled the room, so I also knew they had me surrounded.

"Hey Queenie," a preppy young girl said to me. "I'm sure we have something you could use to cover your body with," she laughed.

"I'm looking for GG," I reasserted.

"Follow me," she directed, walking to the back of the restaurant.

We entered a small office where she handed me a long sleeve button down shirt. It too reeked of feline and it was so strong that it nauseated me. But out of respect, I went ahead and slid into it and took a seat behind the desk.

"Where is GG?" I asked.

"You're speaking to her. And you're sitting in my damn seat."

"A boss should sit at the head of the table, so I took the boss seat," I answered.

She looked at me but kept her comments to herself. "What do you want?"

"I have a small problem that I need a lion to handle. I can't be involved in anyway because it could cost me my life. I can pay any price you ask for," I said, riffling through a stack of papers. As I looked closely I saw their income statement which made me laugh. From the looks of it, they could benefit greatly from a healthy donation.

"What type of problem are you referring to?" she asked, standing up and leaning over the desk. She snatched the paper from my hand and placed it back on the desk, then she took her seat again.

"My husband has brought a human girl into our compound and has made her his second wife. I want her removed and disposed of."

"Why?" she questioned.

"That is none of your business. Either you are going to agree to rid me of this problem or you're not. I can pay any price…money isn't a problem."

"Then if you won't tell me why, tell me who?"

"The human by the name of Ashley."

"Ashley Notah," she repeated. "I will do it for free," she smirked.

"Why for free?" I questioned.

"Because Bullet has an interest in her and she takes his attention away from me. I don't like being number two when I have always been number one," she confessed.

"That is the same issue I'm having," I confided in GG. Since Ashley's arrival my husband has put my emotions and needs on the back burner. The only reason he came to my chambers on the night of his wedding was to witness the birth of his pups. And after he learned of their passing, he ran to be with her. In all actuality he should have been in our chambers, supporting my devastated heart, and helping me to prepare our children for the burial. But that wasn't the case, he ran into the arms of his whore and made her his wife. I heard that even Lilith gave her two gifts that night. The first one made her breast leak in order to feed that monster that I gave birth to and the second gift is that she allowed her to keep the seed that Gethambe had planted into her womb. The second gift is what set this plan into motion because Lilith took my child and added it to her army of Demi-Gods. What a fucking bitch.

"So, how are we going to do this? It's not like the members of the Canine Crew are going to open the gates and allow us access into your city. Especially knowing that we will be there to take Gethambe's precious bride."

"Gather about three other people and I will get you into the compound. But we need to move quickly because Gethambe is not with her right now and this is the perfect time to snatch her from her chambers."

"And how do I know this isn't a trap?"

"You don't. You're just going to have to trust me that I'm telling you the truth."

I then stood up and walked to the door. I took off the shirt and tossed it at GG; I didn't want that smell to linger on my body any longer than it had to.

"Where should we meet you?"

"I don't want you to meet me anyplace. Gather your people and let's go right now," I demanded.

GG got up and followed me out to the main dining area and I noticed as she whispered in the ear of a couple of her people. They all got up from their table and followed me out and to the back of their restaurant.

"Note that once the deed has been done, you will not be able to re-enter at that opening. Not only will it be closed, but a spell will be cast upon it, killing any cat or human that tries to enter."

I then transformed into my wolf and led the pack of cats to the secret tunnel. After we ran though its darkened hallway to the chamber that Ashley resided in, I pushed away a stone and crawled through its opening. Followed by the mountain lions, we entered her room in stealth mode. As they rushed her bed and bound her body in a sheet, I gathered the little princess and handed her to GG.

"What do you want me to do with this?" she questioned.

"Kill it too," I directed.

"Wait a minute," she whispered. "This wasn't part of our bargain."

"Take both of them or neither of them."

She looked at me with disgust as she grabbed the baby from my arms. As she walked back to the opening in the wall, I knocked out Ashley to keep her from making any noises. I quickly made them a sled to place Ashley's body on and hooked it to them while they were in their cat form. Together we raced back to the opening and as I saw them race in the opposite direction of the restaurant, I collapsed the tunnel and used an old spell of protection to give it the illusion that it no longer existed. I also hexed the entrance, causing death to anyone who may stumble near it.

Then I made my way to my chambers and slid back into the room where we bathe. I quickly washed my body just in case Gethambe was to show up so that he couldn't smell the mountain lion's scent on my body.

As I dried my body and made my way to the bed, I heard Gethambe's voice in the hallway. So, I jumped into my bed and pretended to be asleep.

I heard him open the door and close it behind him. I listened as he made his way to my bed and felt the bed shake as he climbed in it with me. Then he scooted his body close to mine and wrapped his arm around my waist and pulled me over to him.

Now this was unusual, I thought to myself. "Take a bath with me," he said.

I pretended to open my eyes from a lazy slumber and look to see his handsome face. I didn't know why he was here or what he wanted, but I figured I would play along with his cute little game of charades.

"Why?" I asked. "Your half-breed bitch on her menstrual?"

"No. I just made love to Ashley last night and Lilith blessed her and allowed her to keep my child," he said. Hearing those words crushed my heart.

"Then why are you in here with worthless little ole me?" I could feel my heart aching knowing that she would soon take my place. "Did you come in here just so that I can wash her climax from your dick?"

"No," he answered, giving me a gentle kiss on my lips. "I came in here to apologize again for all the wrong that I have done to you. I really do love you, Lana."

I turned my back to him and tried to ignore him. But he scooted closer to me and pushed his hardness against my ass. He felt so good and so strong; he was making me cream without being inside of me.

"Why are you in here with me instead of in Ashley's room wooing her?" He couldn't have found out that quick that I had disposed of my problem.

He began to dry hump against my ass as he licked gently on my neck. "I know I have been unbearable to deal with, and I'm sorry for that. I was stressed." He continued to shower the back of my neck with kisses.

"Really?" I asked, getting into the mood.

"Really," he confirmed. "And I want you to know that even if Ashley has a son, her child would not be heir to the throne, our first son will. As a matter of fact, they would rule equally as brothers. And know that you will always be my first wife. Although I love her, you were bred for this and you know how we operate. I just want you to include Ashley and take her under your wing. Teach her how to be a great queen like yourself," he said.

Gethambe was a little too late to give me that piece of news. Yeah, now I felt like shit but what is done, is done. Besides, he didn't know that I personally had a hand in her disappearance. As a matter of fact, when he finds out, I could always say that I was in the bed making love to him.

"You mean that?" I asked, playing the role of a gracious wife.

"Every word of it," he replied. "Now take a bath with me. I know you're sharing me with another woman, but I don't think you want her juices playing chase inside of you with yours."

I got out of the bed and pulled him along with me. As we made our way to the hot springs, we peeled our clothes from our bodies. When we were naked, we submerged ourselves into the hot waters and he took the time to wash my body. I enjoyed his masculine hands as they explored every inch of my body, gently rubbing the soap over it.

When he finished washing my body, I rinsed myself off and watched him as he washed every inch of his. Taunting me, he took his time, especially when he handled his hardness. I couldn't help but smile at him, as he seductively moved his body to entice my eyes.

"You just gave birth to pups. Can we even have sex?" he questioned.

"I can't, but I can ensure that I make you cum."

He rinsed his body and swam over to where I was perched on the side of the hot spring bathing hole. He pulled me down, back into the water and spun me around. "You have two more holes that I can enter…with your permission," he laughed.

This was something that we have never attempted before. His dick was massive, and I was even scared to let him try. If he ripped my pussy a part, just imagine what he would do to my ass.

"I don't know about that one, My Love," I answered.

"Just relax," he said. Then he pushed me forward as he rimmed my asshole with the head of his dick.

Thinking about him entering me from behind was making me go into a full fledge panic attack. My heart was racing, and my breathing became labored. Then he pushed in and I screamed for mercy.

"Gethambe! NOOOO!"

He pulled out and rested his body against mine, holding me tight. I could feel his teeth as his fangs began to extend. I could feel his nails as his claws began to dig into my skin. And then he emitted a soft howl. I knew then that I would have to fight with his beast.

"I want to be inside of you, Lana," he huffed. "I need you."

I turned and looked at him. I kissed his lips and sucked passionately on his fangs, giving them both the same amount of equal attention. I then pushed him back to the stairs that led down into the hot springs and pushed him into a sitting position.

I kneeled in front of him and grabbed his manhood. While continuing to look at him, I started with a slow and passionate suck as I massaged his shaft. I slid my hands up and down its length while slowly twisting my hand when I reached the top.

"Give me you," he begged. "You don't take it down your throat deep enough to give me the sexual gratification I need."

Although I knew I shouldn't have, I gave in to his demand. I stood up in front of him and sat slowly onto his lap. At first, I ground slowly against it, igniting the fire between us. I wanted him as much as he wanted me.

I then grabbed his hardness and slid down its length. As I descended onto it, Gethambe exhaled, closed his eyes, and nestled his head onto my breast. He cupped my ass and squeezed it firmly. I wrapped my arms around his neck and begin to slide my hips forward and backwards, slowly and passionately. While I rode him at a slow and intimate pace, her pushed up into my core.

I could feel as it pulsated inside me, making my body explode with a million shivers of desire. Feeling him as he pushed deep into my soul made me thank the Gods for creating such an amazing man.

Before we could rekindle our bond, my brother came charging into our private bath.

"We need to talk, Gethambe," he said, looking at me as if he knew my dirty little secret.

Gethambe continued to push up in me as he took one of my breasts into his mouth. As if my brother wasn't staring at us as while we continued to sex each other, I continued to ride my husband's hardness.

"Ashley's gone," he blurted. He sparked Gethambe's attention but that didn't stop him from trying to reach his destination.

"Gone where?" he growled. I could feel him begin to swell inside me. I started to increase my pace, taking all of him with ease.

"If I knew, Your Highness, I wouldn't be bothering you while you were digging deep into my sister," he answered.

"She couldn't have gone far," I stated, feeling my blood warm and my lady tingle. I was on the crest of an eruption and I knew that I would become pregnant if I could make my husband release inside of me as well.

"Gethambe…Ashley isn't in the compound," he announced, making Gethambe quit his quest for sexual gratification. Instantly, I could feel his hardness soften and see his face fill with concern.

"What in the fuck do you mean that she isn't within the compound!" he yelled at Rouge.

"Before coming in here to interrupt you, I had the compound thoroughly searched. Not only is she missing, but your daughter is missing too."

He pulled me off his dick and sat my body on the side of him. Gethambe quickly washed himself up and left me sitting in the bath alone. *Damn Rouge*, I thought.

When Gethambe walked out, Rouge stayed behind to speak with me privately. I could tell that he knew that my hands were soiled in this, but he had no proof.

"Please tell me that you didn't do something that you will regret later," he whispered.

"Why would I do something to her?" I snapped.

"Because she threatens your position as first wife. Although you have been locked in this room, I'm sure you knew that Lilith allowed her to keep her first seed."

"And what does that have to do with me?" I asked nonchalantly. I walked out of the warm bath and wrapped myself with a towel.

"Everything," he answered. "It has every fucking thing to do with you."

"Let's go Rouge!" Gethambe yelled out for him.

He looked at me again and pointed his finger at me. "I will kill you myself if you did anything that will disgrace our family name," he spat angrily.

I watched him as he walked out the door, but I held no fear in my heart. There was no way that this could be linked to me. I had been locked in my room to prepare my dead sons for their funeral. And because GG wanted to rid herself of the problem as much as I did, I knew that she would take that secret to her grave.

~~~~~~~~~~~~~~~~~

Chapter Two

Ashley

I woke up feeling slightly dizzy and confused about what had just happened to me. As my vision began to focus and the room stopped spinning, I took a glance at my surroundings to find out I wasn't in my room, in my bed, beside my new husband. Although I was still in my sheer robe, I wasn't in the comforts of my chambers. This place was cold and dark; I believed that I was imprisoned in some sort of cave or ancient building.

Beside me in my bed, my daughter Serenity lay there sleeping peacefully. Neither of us had been harmed. As I pulled the blanket backwards, I noticed that the furniture within this cavern was the furniture from my bedroom. It had been decorated exactly the way I had it in my home. *What the fuck is going on?* I thought to myself.

I pulled my daughter close to me. As she got closer to my breast, she opened her mouth and moved her head around eagerly. I knew that she was ready to feed. So, I laid on my side and opened my gown and placed one of my breasts into her mouth. Hungrily she latched on and began to suck vigorously. I used my finger to stroke the side of her cheek while she fed, giving her a little attention and comfort. I knew that she could feel my emotions, so I didn't want her to feel how terrified I was.

As I lay there feeding my beautiful baby girl, I reminisced about the vows I said to Gethambe, the vows he said to me, how it was me that he ran to when he needed a mother for Serenity, how he made love to me, and how Lilith left my newly fertilized seed as a gift. Everything about that night was perfect; I had finally found happiness. Now, my heart is breaking because I am without the love of my life.

As I pulled Serenity from one of my breasts and placed her on the other one, I tried to remember anything that could give me a clue to what happened. But nothing rang a bell; not to mention that the dead silence that engulfed this room made it hard to think. The only sound came from the sucking noise my daughter made and the dripping of water. I heard no voices, no one walking...nothing.

When Serenity finished feeding and was sleeping peacefully, I lay her small body on her side, propped up with a soft pillow. I covered her with the blanket and eased out of the bed. I needed to explore the confinements of my prison and see if I could get the attention of my captor.

I walked around and found a door, but to my displeasure, it didn't lead outside of my room, but to a bathroom. As I looked more closely at my surroundings, I found that I wasn't in a cave but perhaps some type of ancient temple because it seemed as if the walls were made of limestone. *Where in the fuck am I?* I wondered.

I made my way back to the bed and sat there trying to recall the events that happened after I nestled my body into Gethambe's arms. Then, I heard the main door unlock and looked up to see Bullet. I should have known that he was behind my kidnapping. He wanted me in the worst way and he wanted to hurt Gethambe for stealing my heart.

I leaped from the bed and ran over to him. I immediately started swinging my fist wildly, hitting him in the face and slamming them against his chest. I was mad, hurt, confused, and weak. This event had taken its toll on my body and he knew it.

"What have you done, Bullet?" I cried. "This is going to start a war between the two species!"

"No, Mon Cheri," he said; his voice was calm and soothing. "We have been in a war for many years now. We are now in the uprising stage of this battle."

"Gethambe will kill you," I said, leaning into him and resting my head against his chest. Although I loved Gethambe with all my heart, I have come to appreciate the friendship I had found in Bullet. I didn't want any harm to come to him. I loved the hardness in Gethambe, the possessiveness in his nature, but I appreciated the softness of Bullet.

"Why would he do such a thing when it was my people who saved your life?" he asked, looking at me with confusion in his eyes.

"Didn't you have the baby and I kidnapped?" I asked, looking at him with tear-filled eyes.

"No. No. No, Mon Cheri. Lana allowed GG into your private chambers while you slept and asked her to kill you and the pup. Instead of taking you to the desert and cutting off your head, she brought you back here," he explained.

"So, I'm not a prisoner?"

"You're allowed to walk all around the city. No harm will come to you here. These people see you as their missing link; their connection to the Gods," he explained. Then he reached for my necklace and showed me how it glowed constantly. It was a dull golden glow, but it was illuminated.

"So, I'm free to leave? I'm free to go back to my husband?"

"I wouldn't say that," he smiled. "You're free to walk around your city and see your people. You can take your place here as queen and we can begin to rebuild what we had lost so many years ago."

"In other words, my daughter and I are prisoners?" I said, backing away from him.

"It's not me that is going to hold you here, Mon Cheri. It's the energy of the ancient city, Alexandria. It needs you here to replenish its strength. And until the city has been completely rejuvenated, it's going to hold your essence here. You have the blood of the Gods running through your veins."

"I don't understand," I confessed. "I'm just plain ole Ashley. A successful business woman from Jacksonville, Florida. What do you mean I have the blood of a God?"

"Take a walk with me outside your chambers," he invited.

"My daughter is sleeping, and I can't just leave her in here alone."

"I'll watch her," GG offered. "It has been awhile since we have had the pleasure of having a newborn around here."

I didn't know GG and really didn't trust her with a wolf pup. I didn't want to come back and find my daughter had *accidentally been dropped on her head*...or something. Plus, her personality was too high spirited, and she bounced around all over the place as if she was on some sort of drugs.

"Serenity will be okay. When we were punished, the Gods took away our rights to reproduce. So, the women are going to fall head over heels when they see her. I promise that she is going to have the princess life here, even if she remains a wolf pup."

"What does that mean? Bullet please stop talking to me in riddles. Just say what it is that you're trying to say...fuck...spit it out!" He was really beginning to get under my skin. I didn't want to be here, I missed my husband, and I was still shocked that they had broken into my home and stolen my things.

"Just change your clothes and take a walk with me. All can be explained then. I promise," he guaranteed me.

I walked over to the dresser and pulled out a sundress. I didn't bother looking for a pair of panties or a bra because I knew everyone could smell my aura anyway. So, what would be the use?

I took my robe off and dropped it to the floor, looking at Bullet as I did it. I could see the bulge in his pants and the desire in his eyes as he watched my every movement. I loved being a bitch like that, showing him the very thing that he couldn't have.

"I wish you would open your eyes and appreciate what you could have right here with me. Gethambe has a wife, a daughter that you didn't give him, money, and now...a second wife. I am so envious of his accomplishments."

"Maybe you could learn how to be a boss like him and then all the women will come running to you," I snapped.

"Mon Cheri, you're nothing more than his sloppy seconds...his personal chamber whore to fuck when he gets tired of smelling Lana," he blurted out. I cannot deny that his words were cold and harsh. And that they made my heart shatter into a billion pieces because although I wanted to believe otherwise, he was speaking the truth.

"Where are we going, Bullet? I demanded to know as I walked towards him.

He looked at me hungrily and grabbed me by my hand. We walked out the door and into a great room. There I saw two massive statues, one of a panther and the other of a wolf. They both stood strong, in a warrior's stance. Both were equally beautiful and made of pure gold. At the head of the room sat three large thrones, with the one in the middle being the largest.

"Let me guess, the middle one was for the king and the other two for his two wives?"

"No, Mon Cheri. There sat your ancestor Queen Sheba and she had two husbands. Our society was reversed. We were led by women, not men," he laughed.

Now he had my attention. I wouldn't mind having two husbands and having them cater to my needs daily. Bullet could see the eagerness in me and pulled me away from the throne room and out of the door to look at their lands. I noticed that we were standing in the door of a great temple and it seemed to be placed directly in the center of their society.

"This used to be the most beautiful place in the world. Everything was alive and green. We were surrounded by fertile lands and the Eternal Nile. When Sheba denied the hand of my father and chose her second husband, King Noel, he gave his life to Lucifer and the Gods took away our blessings. They too felt that she should have taken my father's hand in marriage."

"And why didn't she?"

"Because she was in love with a wolf. The heart wants what the heart wants, Mon Cheri. Besides, my father was a cruel and hateful man. He ruled this place with an iron fist. Not to mention that he refused to be beneath a woman," he smiled. But I could see through his fake smile and could feel the heartache.

"So, what happened to Queen Sheba and her followers?"

"Queen Sheba ran off many years ago with her true love, King Noel. By her being of cat origins, she was to marry a lion, panther, tiger…a cat. And she did. But she also wanted to put King Noel on her right side which was a big no – no for our kind. Back then, there was no mingling of the bloodlines."

"And what about now?"

He looked at me and laughed. "Well, you're living proof that it has happened. I am mesmerized by you because I can smell the sweet essence of your inner cat. Gethambe is mesmerized by you because he can smell the sweet essence of your inner wolf. And we both are captivated by the succubus blood that flows rampant throughout your body."

I looked out onto the wasteland, watching the people as they paraded around happily. They didn't have much, but these people were happy. But what boggled my mind was, these people were of different species. As I looked upon them further, I noticed that there were a variety of cats and some wolves. Some were in their beast while others were walking around in their human form.

"Explain to me my history," I said.

"Walk with me."

I didn't answer him but followed close behind Bullet. He led me down the steps and through the city. Before long, we were walking down a dirt path to what looked like a dried-up river of some sort.

"Touch the ground," he directed.

I kneeled on the ground, picked up a hand full of dried sand, and allowed it to trickle back down to the ground. Something about its texture made me want to cry. So, I dug my fingers into it and just waited.

My body was overcome by a tranquil feeling. I could feel the cool breeze as it blew through my hair, feel the sun as it warmed my skin, and became in tuned with the nature that surrounded me. I could feel the life all around me, how it needed me, how it wanted me.

I closed my eyes and saw visions of my ancestor Sheba and her mother, Lilith. I watched how she was torn from her mother's arms and given to the Gods to raise as their own. Her mother became Charmeine, the angel of harmony and her father, Michael, the angel of loyalty. I watched as she fed from her mothers' breast, as she grew and fought as a fierce warrior with the wolves, and I watched her affection grow towards her forbidden love interest. I could see my past and all the members of our family. This blood laid dormant in my people for so long…until I returned to Arizona. The land had woken my spirit and drew two men toward me for my heart.

When I opened my eyes, I could see as the Eternal Nile began to fill. It wasn't something that would happen overnight, but it was beginning to have life. I also noticed that spot in which I sat had begun to grow grass.

"As I stated before, you were meant to be here. Not with the wolves. Your essence gives Alexandria life."

"I saw visions of Queen Sheba and her being pulled from her mother's arms. Why was she taken?" I asked.

"Legend states that Lilith was punished for not submitting to her husband Adam, in the Garden of Eden. So, she ran away and hid in a cave. When Adam went to the Almighty and told him of her unwillingness to submit, the Almighty cursed her womb. But somehow, she was able to have one child with her new husband, Samael. And when the

Almighty heard of this, the child was taken and given to the angels. Although Alexandria had been destroyed many years ago, it was rebuilt for the lions to call home."

"So why didn't Lilith or Samael come back and claim their daughter?" I wanted to know.

"Because this city is cloaked and so was Sheba. Our city lies between two realms. We will never be found because our lands are in the Eternal Realm of Life. But when the gates are opened to leave and enter the living world of Earth, we become visible for only a few moments."

"Now if that is true, how do they find their way back?" I snickered. I have heard a lot of tall tales, but that one took the cake.

"I can't explain it," he answered. "It's like our spirit brings us back to our home."

"With that being said, are you telling me that not only is your land holding me against my will, but my husband will never find me unless someone brings him to me?" I asked with tears swelling in my eyes and my heart sinking deep into my stomach.

"That is correct, Mon Cheri," he answered.

I stood up and looked at him with sorrowful eyes. I couldn't get over all that I had learned. From Lana trying to have Serenity and I killed, my soul belonging to this cursed land, to the possibility of never seeing my husband again. I didn't ask for this life and I didn't want it if it was going to cost me my relationship with the only man who truly loved me.

Bullet pulled me into him and tried to give me some comfort. And I would be lying if I told you that he didn't feel good or right; because he did. As he wrapped his arms around my body and swayed with it, I became relaxed. Without warning, I noticed my body beginning to change. My skin darkened, turning as black as tar, and my nails grew long and sharp. They glistened like the sun, as they turned solid gold.

I stepped back and saw that I had become a panther. I still had some human features, but I was mostly feline. I twisted my body to see my long tail as it peeked from under my sundress. I was amazed with the fact that I was able to wiggle it.

Bullet turned into his mountain lion and gave me a sweet embrace. *"We were meant to be,"* he said to me telepathically.

"Although I am feline, my heart belongs to Gethambe. It always has, and it always will," I answered him.

"I believe that in time, you will learn to love and appreciate me. I will be the man that you have sitting on your

right side. I am intelligent, kind, calm, and very affectionate. I am even willing to help you raise your pup. Anything to be with you, Mon Cheri."

   "I love that you offer me so much, but I can't offer you what I don't feel. Please don't let this ruin our friendship," I begged him. I was just coming into my new self and what I really needed was some time and space.

   As I made my way back to the temple, all of those that I passed, bowed to me. Behind me, I left a trail of new grass and flowers. The land was beginning to awaken, and I was beginning to accept who I was.

<div align="center">~~~~~~~~~~~~~~~~~~~~</div>

Chapter Three

Bullet

Since Ashley's arrival, our lands have rapidly improved, and her willingness to help has been astonishing. But I can still see her pain; we all feel it. When she cries at nights in her chambers, it rains. Her feelings are controlling our weather. Not to mention that Serenity is growing faster than what we had anticipated. That within itself is stressful. Every day it seems that she has aged. A couple of days ago, she was still feeding from Ashley, now she's up and crawling around all over the place.

I felt that Ashley wanted to stay with us, but I know her heart yearns for Gethambe. It's funny how history has a way of repeating itself. Her ancestor loved a wolf and so does she. I hate knowing that her fate will end like that of Queen Sheba. It wasn't until she escaped this place that she was able to have her happy ending.

Today, I thought about taking Ashley over to the exotic gardens that now have life and giving her a break from her daughter and the community's constant demands. Every day she is using her essence to rejuvenate something for someone and I know she must be tired.

When I entered the temple, which was full of lionesses asking for a blessing of fertility, I eased my way through the pack of women until I had Ashley within my sights. I moved close to her and whispered in her ear, "I want to take you someplace quiet and beautiful."

With Serenity sitting in her lap, she held her hand up and silenced the room. "Good people of Alexandria, my body is exhausted, and I need to give it a break. Please come back tomorrow with your request," she said to them.

When the room was cleared, she yelled for GG to come and take Serenity. I noticed how much she had become dependent on their friendship and instantly thought that once we returned from our evening out, that I may be able to put a bug in her ear about helping me get just as close to Ashley as she was.

"Do I need to shift into my cat?"

"Nah, Mon Cheri. Let's take a walk and enjoy the Almighty's beautiful day."

She stood up and held her hand out for me to hold. But as we made our way to the door, she allowed me to wrap my arm around her.

"I have a secret that I neglected to tell you," she began to confess.

"What is that?" I asked.

"I am carrying Gethambe's baby. I think that there is only one but I'm not for sure. And although this has only happened a couple of days ago, I feel like I can feel it kicking."

"Females in the wolf pack stay pregnant for about eight weeks to nine weeks. And if it is taking the feline traits, you could stay pregnant for as long as four months."

"And what about the human or Demi-God in me?"

"I'm not sure. I guess if your child takes the Demi-God traits, you could stay pregnant for at least six months and the human traits – nine. I have no clue because we haven't been faced with anything like this before," I answered. I was feeling overwhelmed with dread. No wonder she didn't want me, she had consummated her marriage and had been blessed with a baby. What are the odds.

But as I thought about it more, it finally made sense to me why Lana would want Ashley out of the picture. Before we approached the botanical gardens, I stopped her in her tracks and swirled her body around to face me.

"Serenity is Lana's daughter by birth. Right?"

"Yes," Ashley answered, stunned by the seriousness in my voice.

"And how did you end up with her?"

"On my wedding night, Lana gave birth but refused to bond with her. Gethambe brought her to me and asked if I would be her mother. Lilith gave me the ability to feed her and the rest is history," she answered nonchalantly.

"A wolf never has only one pup. What happened to the others?"

"Serenity was an only child I do believe. She was the only one that was given to me."

I didn't want to startle her any further than what I had already, so I dismissed her naïve notion that Serenity was an only child. I opened the door and placed my hand in the small of her back and escorted her inside the botanical gardens.

Everything within these walls had life, from the plants to the ponds and even the colorful butterflies that flew freely around the dome. Before Ashley had graced our lands with her presence, nothing grew, and nothing was fertile. Now we are able to grow some food and one of our own lionesses is pregnant with cubs. We hadn't laid our eyes on a lioness cub in decades.

"It's beautiful," she exclaimed, throwing her arms around my neck and showering me with passionate kisses. I didn't read too much into it, because I wasn't the one holding the keys to her heart.

"Go," I told her. "Run free and relax your weary body."

As the excitement grew in her eyes, she turned to the gardens and shifted into her cat. Then she leaped into the dense plants and flowers and chased after the butterflies. I sat on a bench and watched as she played like a young kitten.

But I knew now that I would have to send a team to bring Gethambe to our city. Not because I wanted him to rekindle his bond with Ashley, but I thought he should know that the woman that he was mated with tried to kill the woman I loved.

Thinking about her carrying his seed made my stomach ball up in knots. That should be my child in her stomach and together we should be rebuilding these lands. I should be the king sitting on her right side, protecting Ashley and enforcing her laws. But because I allowed Gethambe to slither his way into her life, she chose him instead of bonding with me.

As she continued to play chase, I flipped on my mental switch and excluded everyone from my mind except, GG. *"I have a favor to ask you."* I wasn't worried about Ashley finding out that I was having a private conversation about her. Because unlike the wolves, we could flip our switches while still having a conversation and not making any sudden gestures.

"*What is it?*" she replied.

"*I know that what I'm about to ask you can cost you your life, but I need you to retrieve Gethambe for me and bring him here to Alexandria.*"

"*Are you out of your fucking mind, Bullet? Even with a skilled team of soldiers, there is no way in hell that I could get close enough to him to snatch him up and bring him here. This is not like taking candy from a baby...nowhere close!*"

"*But if you take Fatima with you and explain to him that Ashley is in danger, he will come.*"

"*And how in the hell do you know that?*"

"*Because if the roles were reversed, I would go.*"

"*If you're wrong, he will kill me, Bullet.*"

"*But if I'm right and he comes, Ashley could perhaps persuade his way of thinking.*"

"*Now that's bullshit, and you know it. Gethambe is an arrogant asshole with an aggressive attitude. He might love Ashley, but he loves himself more. Gethambe is all about his traditions.*"

"I really need you to do this for me. And know that if we make Ashley happy, she will stay and make us happy. Perhaps even giving you the gift of pregnancy."

GG was quiet, more than likely thinking about the potential of being a mother. Or maybe she was thinking about the dangerous mission I was sending her on.

"I will do it, not for the promise of a child, but for the hope of our future," she finally answered. *"How do I get him to come here without him killing me or Fatima?*

"By telling him Ashley needs him."

"We all know that he is not going to come alone. More than likely he's going to demand that we bring his faithful sidekick Rouge.

"Then bring Rouge but tell them, for your safety, they are going to have to agree to be handcuffed and slightly tranquilized."

"What in the fuck are you smoking? You really think he is going to allow us to drug him? Really, Bullet? And then bring him here, where he doesn't have the backing of his thugs? And you feel that he is going to do all this just to see Ashley?"

"She's pregnant, GG."

There was a moment of silence again. I knew that the news had put her into a state of shock and I believe that she was now reassessing the entire situation.

"When do you want us to leave?" she questioned.

"Immediately. Tell Lala to watch after the baby and that we will be there soon. Also pass around to the people that Gethambe may be coming here to visit but that nobody will be harmed.

"Okay."

"Be careful and come back the same way you're leaving...in one piece."

I looked around to find out where Ashley had disappeared to. She was just prancing around, playing with the butterflies, but now there was silence. I got up from the bench and begin to search for her.

"Ashley!" I yelled out.

She didn't answer me. But as I walked deeper into the green lush green garden of plants and flowers, I felt a stabbing sensation in my back. Ashley had pounced on me, not realizing her cat strength. I flipped my body around and shifted into my lion. Within seconds, I had flipped her around onto her back and I was hovering over her. As I looked into her eyes, I became united with her soul. As we imprinted on

46

each other, her eyes turned Persian blue, and her body inadvertently shifted back into her human body.

I shifted back into my human and lifted myself from her body. But with her nakedness sitting beside me and her scent invading my nostrils, I couldn't control my sexual desire for her. I pulled her body to me and sat her up onto my lap. She cupped my face with her hands and pulled me in for a sweet and gentle kiss.

"Gethambe wouldn't approve," I whispered to her as she sucked softly on my bottle lip.

"He has nothing to worry about," she assured.

I noticed that her eyes were sporadically changing colors. They went from soft hazel color to Persian blue; from a Persian blue to an emerald green, and they stayed that color as she examined my face intimately. And then she did the unexpected, she began to suck the life from my body. It was her succubus revealing herself to me.

I tried to push her away, but her demon was strong. She was grinding wildly against my hardness while sucking my essence from my body.

"You're hurting me," I whispered. Normally it wouldn't be a problem for my kind to feed her demon, but it works better when you're engaged in a sexual act. As they are drawing sexual gratification from your essence, your energy is being returned to you from her spirit. But I dared not enter her body while she was pregnant with Gethambe's child. That would definitely bring about a great war.

Ashley heard my plead and released her hold on me. She looked at me confusingly as she pulled her nakedness off my lap. Her cream had begun to spill and the scent of it drove me crazy with want. I rose to my knees and grabbed her by the hips and pulled her close to me. I rubbed my nose in her sacred garden and flickered my tongue across her nub. She tossed one leg over my shoulder and pulled my head closer to her body.

As she swirled her hips passionately, I licked and bathed her sweet little lady. She was grinding hard against my tongue, riding it like a surfboard. When her cream began to spill from her, I drank it up like a smooth cup of wine. I didn't allow one drop to go to waste.

"Uhm," she moaned, enjoying her slow descent into euphoria.

"Are you good?" I growled, knowing that she was but I wasn't. My dick was hard, and it ached for her.

"Yes," she answered. "But what am I going to do about you?" she inquired.

"Nothing. I'm just going to have to massage one out. As much as I hate Gethambe, I would never disrespect him like that," I told her.

She pulled her leg down and walked over to a small stone wall and sat down on it. Ashley opened her legs wide and began to play blissfully with her nub. "Play with it in front of me," she demanded. "And when you think you are about to explode, let me know."

I didn't know what type of game she was playing, but it didn't matter. My dick was hard, and it was begging for a sweet release, even if I had to help myself achieve it.

I stood in front of her and stroked my hardness as she caressed my balls. Slowly, I slid my hand up and down the length of my manhood, squeezing it tightly for a little extra pleasure. Ashley would lean in every so often and stick out her tongue and roll it around the tip of my hardness, making sure that she was sucking up the precum.

Feeling her soft and warm lips suck on the head sent a tsunami of shimmering delight racing throughout my body. As the excitement built, my heartbeat quickened, my blood warmed, and my balls tightened.

"It's coming, Baby," I warned her. "It's coming."

Ashley moved my hand and took me deep down her throat. I was so excited that I couldn't pull it out of her mouth. Instead, I grabbed the back of her head and began to push passionately into her mouth. I was thrusting my hips quickly, enjoying the sensual feel of her velvet tongue as she sucked it hard and savagely.

As I felt my eruption pushing out, I flung my body around, pulling it out of her mouth, and shot my warm juices towards the plants. My body jerked wildly as my cum shot violently from my body. When I had finished, I fell down onto my knees and tried desperately to catch my breath. When I looked over at Ashley, her eyes were changing colors again as she watched the show that I had just provided for her enjoyment.

If for no other reason than to help control her succubus, I needed Gethambe here and I needed him here quickly. Otherwise, I was going to end up ramming all this dick into his wife while she was pregnant with his child. Dammit, I wish that was my child growing inside of her inside of Gethambe's.

"We need to get you back to your chambers," I huffed.

"I don't want to go back to my chambers," she snapped. "I want to fuck," she stated. She came toward me and started to circle me as if I were her prey. "Don't you want me?"

"More than the air I breathe. But not here," I lied. "I want to make love to you, not pound mercilessly inside your precious core. You deserve more than that, Mon Cheri."

She smiled as her eyes settled into a soft lavender color. Then she proceeded to the door as I gathered my strength to follow behind her. We made our way to the temple and she dismissed the help and had them take Serenity with them. They gathered their things and hurriedly left the room. They had seen this many times before when Sheba's succubus first emerged. They understood the lust that she had built up and if she didn't release it soon, she would begin to feed on whoever was near her. It didn't matter if it was male or female, she would indulge in her sexual feeding frenzy until she became sexually satisfied. The only people that were safe from her ravishing appetite were the children and any elder that was sick.

When we entered her bedroom, I had thought about ways to distract her. I started with telling her that I had sent for her husband.

I saw her eyes slowly change to hazel as her demeanor changed. I even saw a quick smile of appreciation on her face.

But soon after seeing that gorgeous smile and enjoying her calming temperament, her smile dissipated. I walked over to her bed, grabbed the sheet and wrapped it around my body. I wanted her to focus her energy someplace other than on my swinging dick.

"What did you say?" she questioned.

"Nothing."

"God that feels so good," she moaned, tilting her head back and pinching her nipples.

"Ashley…are you okay?" I asked, as I slowly backed away from her.

Then she froze; locking her eyes on mine. This time they were solid white, and her skin glowed an eerie color of green.

"I see death. I can feel her fear as her heart begins to slow. She's choking and it's hard for her to breathe. So many tears are falling rapidly from her eyes because she has just learned that she will be denied entrance into the afterlife. Her punishment is to become enslaved to the soul eater for all eternity. Her mother is strong, yet emotionless, as if she is okay with the final judgement. Her father tries to stand strong with the help of his sons, because he genuinely loves her, and it is ripping him apart to stand there and watch her soul being

pulled from her body. There is nothing he can do. Although she is pleading for her life, the demon goddess snatches it from her body and takes it down to Hell with her. There is one person who can save her, but she finds it hard to forgive her actions," Ashley announced.

Her vision took all the energy she possessed. She made her way to the bed and lay across it. "I'm sorry," she apologized.

I didn't care that she attempted to sex me into oblivion, I wanted to know who she saw in her vision. "Ashley, who was being eaten by the demon goddess?" I questioned.

"Lana. Her life will be taken from the Earth realm on the next full moon. Agrat bat Mahlat will suck her soul from her body and feed it to Eisheth Zenunim. I saw Lilith watching, her eyes were filled with satisfaction. Lana's life will be sacrificed because she made an attempt Serenity's and mine," she explained, pulling the blanket up to her neck.

"And who can save her, Mon Cheri?"

"Serenity, but Lana has hardened her heart," she answered, falling into a deep sleep.

Instead of getting in the bed with her, I started a fire and laid on the bear rug. After those two events, I knew that she would sleep for at least two or three days. At least Sheba would. It takes a lot of power to see into the future, it drains the seer mentally, physically, and emotionally. But I welcome the break and can't wait for Gethambe's arrival.

~~~~~~~~~~~~~~~~~~

Chapter Four

Gethambe

As we tried to figure out where the breach in our compound was, we had visitors requesting to enter the golden gates. I was told that it was Fatima and that she was accompanied by a mountain lion. My heart began to pound with anger and hostility knowing that they were able to sneak into my home and kidnap my wife and daughter. I was going to rip Fatima's head off and shove it up her own ass if she didn't tell me what I needed to know. I allowed them entrance but had them escorted to the west conference room. I told the Canine Crew to hold them there until I figured out what was going on.

I had sent a crew to Ashley's home in the city to see if she somehow got out and took the baby out for a while…but there was no way she could leave without somebody noticing her.

"Your Highness, I'm at Ashley's place and I believe that someone has burglarized it," Loc reported.

"What do you mean?" I asked.

"First of all, her front door was unlocked.

*Secondly, I'm in her bedroom and everything is missing.
Even the clothes from her closet are gone,"* he answered.
I could hear the panicking in his voice.

"Can you tell if anything else is missing?"

*"It looks like just her bedroom furniture but there
are a bunch of papers scattered all over the place. If I had
to take a guess, whoever was here, they were in a hurry,"*
he replied.

*"Okay. Stay put but keep out of sight. Let me know
if you see anyone going to or from her house. I'm going to
send Joker to help you keep watch over the place,"* I
advised. I pointed to Joker who morphed into his beast and
ran swiftly out of the room.

*"Sir, I can say that there is a heavy smell of
peppermint and lavender. It's so strong that I am unable
to pick up a scent of any mountain lion that may be
nearby,"* Loc informed me.

I looked at Rouge who looked back at me. At the
same time, we said, "Bullet."

"Rouge, you got my back?"

"From the womb to the tomb, my nigga. Tell me

when to jump and I'm all over that ass," he answered.

"Let's go have a small talk with Fatima and that pussy bitch she has with her," I demanded.

I tried to keep up the appearance that I wasn't worried, but Rouge could see through that charade and could tell that I wasn't in a good place. Truth was, my heart had slid down through my intestines and fell out of my ass. Something about this whole situation reeked that Lana was somehow involved.

As we started toward the conference room Rouge said, "I can hear your thoughts even with your switch flipped. You're thinking that my sister has something to do with Ashley's disappearance."

"I do," I answered him honestly. He was more than just a loyal soldier, he was my best friend. Someone I could trust with my deepest secrets without worrying about them coming back to haunt me.

"Do you think that she feels that Ashley's pregnancy is threating her position?" he inquired.

"If she did, she doesn't anymore. I told her today that she would always be the first wife and that our first son would have his share of the throne. I am doing my best to do right by them both. I love Lana just like I love Ashley. It's just that your sister can be so damn evil sometimes," I joked.

"She isn't shit compared to my mother," he laughed.

"On a different note, I need to ask you something."

"Anything," Rouge stated.

"Where does your loyalty lie, Rouge? If it is found out that your sister has played a part in Ashley's disappearance, the elders are going to probably have her killed. And there is nothing I can do to stop them."

He stopped walking and looked me straight in my eyes and said, "For real my nigga? You need to ask me a bitch ass question like that? I'm loyal to my king and my tradition…just like my father. If my sister is wrong and she must be punished, all I can do is pray that the Gods would show my sister some mercy. I would hope that they would at least allow her to go through reincarnation and get a second chance at life," Rouge answered. I could hear the sincerity in his voice and I could also tell that I had offended him by questioning his honor.

"I'm more than just your King...bitch boy. I'm your brother from another mother. And I would understand if you hated me for all that I have done to your sister. She's a good woman and she didn't ask for this. And to keep it one hundred, I don't know what I would have done if she came to me talking about bringing another man into our home and marrying him. You know me, I'm selfish. I don't share and don't play well with others," I said. We both laughed but changed our demeanor once we reached the conference room. With Rouge at my side, accompanied by Stewart and Juice, we were ready to mop the floor with these bitches.

As we entered, Juice and Stewart manned the door while I took a seat at the head of my table with Rouge sitting on my right-hand side. I had no idea what type of trickery these bitches were up to, but I was ready to face the music.

I knew that Fatima held hostile feelings against our people because she was kicked out after losing the battle to Lana. But she knew that was a possibility when she signed up for the fight. If she won, her life would have been taken but she would have been assured a place in Edom and given a respectable position amongst their society. But if she lost, after all the years of training that she had received from this tribe, she would be shunned.

If shunned, we provide our warriors with enough money and food to live comfortably amongst the humans. Besides, once you are kicked from the compound, you are also stripped of your immortality, so Fatima wouldn't have any problem fitting in with the commoners.

As I stared at Fatima, a chambermaid walked over to me. She bowed and then asked, "Would you like something to drink, My Lord?"

"Yeah, bring me a shot of Bullet, the red label," I answered.

"May I have a double shot of that," Rouge asked.

She nodded her head and scurried off to grab our drinks.

Before we could get our drinks, Samael and his wives shimmered into the conference room and took a seat at the table. I knew then that the shit was about to hit the fan.

When they pop in unannounced like that, they usually bring bad news with them.

"Oh, how sweet," Samael said, smiling at Fatima. "I see you finally gave in to your desires and started playing with pussy." We all laughed at his joke.

She didn't acknowledge Samael and I could tell that she didn't find his humor amusing. She just kept her focus on me along with her new kitty cat friend.

"Where is she?" Lilith asked.

Fatima didn't acknowledge Lilith either. She looked at me and said, "Ashley is safe, and no harm will come to her if you agree to take a small journey with us…peacefully."

"What the fuck!" I allowed my emotions to show. My voice was loud, and it echoed throughout the room scaring the chambermaid who was bringing our drinks. Hearing my voice made her drop the glasses onto the floor.

"Ashley is having the time of her life," the preppy little mountain lion stated. "Bullet is keeping her, and the baby entertained," she smirked.

I stood up and leaped in her direction to be held back by my loyal soldiers. She had touched a nerve in me that made my blood boil with rage. As they got me back into my seat, the little bitch laughed.

"Fatima. You have two choices. One, you can take me to my wife or two, I can allow Rouge to get the information I need from you and then I will have you and your little pussy diposed of," I demanded, slamming my fist against the table.

Before she could answer, Lana walked into the room to find out what was going on. Without warning, Lilith sprung to her feet and had began to choke the life from Lana's body. Stewart and Juice tried to pull her from Lana, but she had the power of a God; she was unmovable.

"SIT!" I heard Samael yell out. His voice was like thunder as it shook the walls and ground.

Lilith let Lana go and took her seat. Lana fell to the floor and grabbed her neck. She could barely breathe.

"Foolish, jealous, queen!" Lilith yelled out. "He chose you and your unborn seed, not Ashley's. But you just couldn't wait...could you?"

"What are you talking about?" Lana cried.

"Because you endangered my bloodline, I curse your

body the way that the Almighty cursed mine. You will never be able to bear children. And the one child that survived, you will never see again," Lilith hexed Lana.

"Young queen. I wish we could have met on better terms, but unfortunately for you, today is not a good day to play stupid with the Gods. I knew what you were going to do before you did it. Now, you will pay for it with your life."

"I didn't do anything," Lana cried. She then sprung up from the floor and ran over to me. "I promise you, My Love. I didn't do anything to harm Ashley. I'm the one who told you to go get her. I'm the one who wanted this union to work. I didn't do anything to our wife," she cried.

I pushed her away and looked at Fatima. "What is it going to take for me to see my wife and daughter again?" I humbled myself.

"The rules are –"

"I didn't give you permission to speak. Be a good little kitty and shut the fuck up. A pussy has no business mingling with the wolves or Gods. Your people lost their voice and privileges a long time ago," I snapped.

"Funny you should say that," she giggled. "Because the last time I saw Ashley, she looked exactly like Queen Sheba. Your precious Ashley is a 'pussy' just like me. Boom Bitch!"

"It is true, My Lord. Ashley has morphed into the mirror imagine of Queen Sheba. I have seen it with my own eyes," Fatima confirmed.

"How could that even be possible?" Lilith questioned. "I am a succubus and my blood is her blood. We don't have cat genes."

"When your daughter fed from the breasts of a God, she was blessed with Demi-God powers. Although she was a true succubus, she inherited the genes of the feline. We have no rational reason why, but it is true. But most importantly, her succubus has shown its face and it needs to be fed. Bullet will not enter her body while she is pregnant with your pups, My Lord."

You could have knocked me over with a cat whisker. I couldn't believe what I had just heard. That my wife was a cat and mirrored Queen Sheba's image. I remember seeing her once as a young pup and her beauty was compared to that of Aphrodite. No woman came close to matching it. I couldn't believe that I had fallen in love with a pussy…literally.

"I didn't see that coming," Samael admitted. "I couldn't sense her feline traits. I could only see the wolf that hid within her."

"So, is she wolf or lion?" Rouge asked.

"I'm going to have to get back with you on that, because I'm not sure. All the visions I had of Ashley I could see her wolf and her succubus only. Nothing I saw said that she had the feline gene," he answered. I could see that Lilith and Samael were puzzled by the news.

"Since you don't know your own history, let a wee pussy cat enlighten you. Lilith, your daughter fed from the breast of an angel which transformed her into the deity that we know as Sheba. She was the most beautiful creature that walked these lands. Her skin was black as tar, she was intelligent, stood tall, and was extremely powerful. The Gods felt that her only downfall was that she fell in love with a wolf. She was denied the union, they ran off together leaving the city of Alexandria to die. So, in short, not only did Sheba leave us for the love of a wolf, but our king, to whom she was promised, left us as well. Leaving our city to crumble and fall," the mountain lion explained.

"Fatima. Tell me how I can see my wife. I don't care that she is a cat…I love and miss her," I pleaded.

"We are willing to take you to her. But there is one condition."

"Anything," I answered.

"You are to be sedated. We need to know that you will not try to attack us."

"Bullshit!" Rouge intervened. "If you think I'm going to allow you to sedate my king and take him to who knows where, you need to rethink that thought."

"You are welcomed to come with him as his protection, but the same applies to you," Fatima answered.

"One go. We all go," Juice chimed in. "Joker is close and will be here in a matter of seconds."

"Nigga speak for yourself. I'm not letting this bitch and her girly friend stick anything into my body. The only sticking that will be going on around here is me shoving this dick up in some mountain lion pussy," Stewart laughed.

Samael looked in his direction and waved his hand. Within a few seconds, Stewart was out cold on the floor. "I couldn't bear to hear his whining and crying any longer. While you are away, I will help Loc maintain order around the compound. I will also be digging into this wonderful tale of Queen Sheba. I need answers. And by the way, until we find out for sure how big of a part Lana played into the capture of Ashley, she will be imprisoned on Edom."

"Let no harm come to her, Demon," I said to Samael.

"Nothing will happen until after you return. You have my word."

As they stood, Lilith rushed to my side and said, "There are a couple of things that you need to know about her succubus. Watch her eyes, they will tell you what she needs. Blue eyes mean that her body is craving, and it should be fed immediately. Green eyes mean that she has been without for too long and it may take two men to satisfy her needs. If her eyes are green, never try to feed her hunger alone. She will kill you. I know that she is pregnant, and you don't want another man to enter her, but there are other ways to satisfy her sexual appetite. Lastly, you will know that she is enjoying it and is completely satisfied when her eyes turn lavender. That is when her succubus has been controlled. But know this, because you are not a God, she will need two husbands to contain her yearning for sex. So, make your peace with that," she warned. "Right now, her craving should be low since she is pregnant, but not even that is a guarantee," she explained.

Then, Samael shimmered away with his four wives and Lana.

I looked at Fatima and asked, "Now how are we going to do this? If you drug us all, there is no way you can get us back to your lands."

"We already thought out a plan," she smiled.

"You all will be drugged, and we will go by horse and buggy across the desert. This is the only way that I will agree to take all five of you. But I need your word that none of these people will be hurt."

"On my word as the king of Achaemenid, no harm will

come to Bullet or his people. We are going there in peace so that I can talk to my wife and see my daughter," I promised.

"One more thing that we forgot to tell you," the mountain lion said. "Ashley cannot leave Alexandria until the land has fully rejuvenated. Alexandria will not release her spirit until then. So, no kidnapping attempts or that too will kill our people."

"What?" I asked. The mountain lion didn't say anything more but asked us to take her to the barn where we kept the royal horses. Her only concern was getting back to her home. I think she had enough of being around the wolves.

~~~~~~~~~~~~~~~~~~~~

Chapter Five

Lana

The Gods have been kind enough not to put me in a prison for common criminals. Because of my status, I have been placed in a mansion while I await my trial. I am not able to leave because this place has a spell of confinement placed on it. So, although people can enter, my body is held hostage. But little do they know; this hexed home doesn't restrict my astral projection ability.

So, as I lay in my bed for the night, my body became frozen in time while my spirit shimmered from it once again. I was looking down onto my body as it floated up to the ceiling and then out of the window. I traveled through a spiral of magnificent rays of vibrant colors, moving at the speed of light, until my spirit arrived in Alexandria. I looked frantically for a host, but was unable to find a suitable animal, so I shimmered into an older woman that had just left a great temple.

I saw GG as she walked with Gethambe and his crew coming toward me. As they passed by, I pretended to fall, knowing that GG would be all too happy to help an elderly lady up. As Gethambe and his loyal soldiers continued to blindly follow Fatima, I snatched GG by the arm and pulled her to the side of the temple steps. I placed an immobility spell quickly to keep her from running or yelling out for help. And then I cast upon her a spell to make her forget about meeting me and helping with the disposal of Ashley and Serenity:

Darkness falls and darkness flows,

The mind is weak and does not know.

Live the lie and remove the deed,

Erase the secret you do not need.

And with a swipe of my hand across her forehead, the encounter that we shared was erased. I removed the immobility spell and scurried away from where she stood. I walked around the village repeating the spell to each of the members that was a part of the kidnapping before releasing my host to continue with her day. I flew back to Edom and back into my body and slept like an angel. I wasn't worried about the Gods finding out what I had done to cause havoc within our society. Without GG or the others, they had nothing on me. *Who is the stupid queen now?* I chuckled to myself as I closed my eyes to get a good night's rest.

I woke the next morning to breakfast in bed. The servant girl was kind enough to make me a traditional breakfast. She scrambled me two eggs, fried some bison meat, and wrapped it in fry bread. On the side she had a variety of fresh picked berries and a large glass of goat milk that was gathered this morning. If this was to be my punishment, I could deal with this. Although I missed my husband, I was so stress free. For the first time in a long time, I felt alive.

After eating my breakfast, I went to the bathroom to get myself cleaned up for the day. Like home, I was provided warm waters from the hot springs that were nearby. I peeled out of my gown and slowly stepped down into the soothing water. Once submerged up to my neck, I closed my eyes and leaned my head backwards into the water.

Although I knew it wasn't washing my sins away, it felt like it. It was like I was floating on a cloud, surrounded by love, peace, and tranquility. It was quiet and pure. And all that I have done in the past had been forgiven. But when I pulled my head out of the water and reopened my eyes, I realized that it was nothing more than foolish hopes. I knew that if I escaped the horrible fate that followed me, I would still be burdened with the trials and tribulations of my earthbound life.

I grabbed a sponge and begin to wash my body. As I touched myself, I thought about Gethambe and how he had a way of making my body submit to him. Once I conquered how to control his beast, he had become an excellent lover. I loved the way he would lick my tears away, hold me tightly in his arms while consoling my fears and uncertainties. I loved the way he filled me up and allowed me to experience multiple orgasms. I just loved him.

But my good mood was soon interrupted as I heard Lilith's voice. "Stupid young queen," she said. "You are going to die for the crime you committed against Ashley." Then she took a seat on the counter as I continued to bathe myself.

I pretended to not know what she was talking

about. I knew they didn't have any proof of my wrongdoings so fuck what she was talking about. There was no way she could get me to tell on myself...I just wasn't that damn stupid.

"Is there something I can help you with, My Lady?" I asked, not even making eye contact with her. She may be a God, but I lacked respect for any woman who had to fuck their way to the top.

"Just tell us what you did and die with honor. I promise to put in a good word for you with my sister wife. Maybe she would allow your soul to remain here in Edom as a servant for her," she snickered.

"My Lady, I have not wronged you in any way. I would have never harmed Ashley," I lied with ease.

Lilith hopped off the counter and made her way to the hot springs where I was bathing. She took off her clothes and stepped down into the bathing hole and swam over to me. She took the sponge from my hand and motioned for me to turn my back to her. Then she soaked the sponge with warm water and squeezed it over my shoulders. She did this several times before whispering in my ear, "I'm not an enemy that you want to have."

"I would never want you as an enemy, My Lady. I know the importance of having you on my side. For that reason, I wanted Ashley to be a part of my family. I would never wish any harm on her," I said.

"You're a foolish queen if you think that I would believe anything that falls from your lips. You felt threatened when all your sons died, and Ashley became pregnant. This would cost you your husband and your crown," she stated, pulling me close to her and kissing me on the back of my neck.

"Gethambe had promised me that our child would reign equally as king alongside his child with Ashley. He had also stated I would never lose my position as first wife because I had trained for this and I am a part of the people," I told her.

"Was that before or after you tried to get rid of my descendant?" she hissed.

"He disclosed that information while he was deep inside of me and while Ashley lay asleep in her room. When he came to visit me that morning, he wanted to make love to me and Gethambe told me that he had just left her chambers. So, riddle me this Lilith, how could I be in two places at one time?" I questioned, as I turned to face my nemesis.

With a wicked smile on my face, I leaned into the Demi-God and gave her a soft, sensual, long, tantalizing kiss. I even went as far as to wrap my arms around her neck and stick my tongue deep down her throat. To me, this was the sweetest revenge that I could offer her. I had left no evidence, and according to my husband's own mouth, I had no reason to bring harm to my sister wife.

She pulled away from me and swam back. "You lie," she whispered.

"No, My Lady, you can verify this with my husband. I was locked in my room and the door was guarded by two of the Canine Crew members. I cleaned my sons as ordered and prepared their bodies for burial. When the undertaker came to my room, I handed them to him and took a quick bath. About an hour or so later, I was laying in the bed with my husband at my side," I explained.

"And he will give us that same story?" she

questioned. I could tell that she was becoming irritated with me. Deep inside of her, she knew that I was being deceitful, but the mounting evidence supported me. And even if GG had told someone her story, she couldn't remember it now and none of the elders knew that I dabbled in black magic. So, there was nothing that they could do to me, and she knew that if Gethambe stated that he was with me when Ashley disappeared, they had to set me free.

"Yes, My Lady. I have no reason to bear false witness. Ashley wasn't a threat to my children, my crown, or my husband. I had no reason to cause her any harm," I explained, swimming over to the steps.

"Then if not you, who?" she asked.

I stepped out of the bathing hole and wrapped a towel around my body. I snapped my fingers and the servant girl came running with another one for Lilith. As she covered her body and we took a seat on the bench in the bathroom, I put the second part of my plan into motion.

"How did Ashley end up in Alexandria?" I asked. "In a place that you cannot see or visit?"

She looked out into space and began to concentrate on the lies that were spilling elegantly from my lips. "So, what are you implying?"

"Nothing, My Lady. All I'm saying is that now Ashley is in Alexandria, the lions are beginning to evolve into a higher species. Remember the warning that little kitty gave Gethambe? Ashley cannot leave until their lands have reached full rejuvenation. So, all I'm saying is that they needed her there far more than I needed her gone," I said with sincerity in my voice.

"That's right," she agreed. "But how would they get into Achaemenid? It's impenetrable."

"We have been under attack for many years," I said. "Who knows if they have found a way to sneak in and out of our compound without notice. The lions aren't as naïve as they want us to believe."

Again, Lilith heard the words that I was saying and thought about them. Everything I was saying to her was making sense and there was no reason for her to doubt my authenticity once I revealed to her what Gethambe had promised me.

I wanted to pat myself on the back because I couldn't have planned this shit out better. Now that I had planted the seed in Lilith's mind, all I had to do was sit back and wait for all the fireworks to kick off.

"I am blinded to Alexandria and its location. Do you know where it is located?" she questioned.

Playing dumb, I answered, "No My Lady. I though Alexandria had been destroyed many years ago. We didn't even know that the mountain lions resided there. But that could be the reason why we could never locate their domicile. The wolves have spent a lot of time trying to search out their home, but we were never able to locate it. But if I had to guess, I don't think it would be on the Earth realm."

She thought for a minute and said, "I would have to ask Samael."

Then I threw in another piece of information to add fuel to the fire. "My Lady, isn't Samael the father of Queen Sheba?"

"Yes. What of it?"

"Then wouldn't he be blinded to Alexandria

location as well? Or maybe he isn't and just didn't want you to know that he knew where your daughter was all this time."

Lilith's skin changed to a candy apple red with her eyes matching. It was quite scary to look at, but I continued to sit on the bench beside her and remained calm. I even pretended to care.

"My Lady, are you okay? Do I need to grab you a glass of water?"

She didn't answer. I could tell she was overcome with rage and she was standing on the peak of her volcano and ready to erupt.

I raced over to the bathing hole and grabbed the sponge. I soaked up the water and then raced back over to her. I squeezed the sponge and allowed the water to trickle out of it and down onto her body. Lilith's body was so heated that the water evaporated quickly, turning to steam.

She stood up and quietly walked out of the bathroom. I followed her through the mansion until she reached the front door. Lilith turned and looked at me with pure fury overtaking her body.

"Edom will not sit quietly today because all hell is about to be unleased."

"My Lady," I said. "Stay for a spell and let's talk about this. You don't want to upset the Almighty."

"The Almighty has cursed my womb and took my only daughter. My husband knew where she resided and neglected to tell me. And now, she is being held hostage against her will. We have nothing more to talk about," she said angrily.

Then she exited the mansion, removing the hex that held me hostage. I raced up the steps and threw on a simple gown. I ran back down the steps and out of the front door. I wanted to see my father, I needed some advice and he was the wisest man I knew.

As I ran through the streets of Edom, I felt the ground quiver beneath my feet. The sky had become dark and it had begun to rain. As children we were taught that when it stormed heavily, and you heard loud thunder, it was due to the Gods fighting. And from the sound of it, Lilith was giving Samael hell.

When I arrived at my parents' home, I beat against

the door with all my might. Once the door opened, I dashed inside and slammed it tightly behind me. I ran through the house until I located my father and I leaped into his arms. I just wanted him to hold me.

"What is it?" he asked concerned. "How did you get out of solitary confinement?"

"Daddy," I cried. "I'm scared. I don't want to die."

"Baby girl," he said. "What did you do?"

"Lilith came for a visit and she thinks I had something to do with Ashley's disappearance. But I didn't. Everything was going great between all three of us. I had no reason to harm her," I lied.

"Then the Gods will see that and set you free," he answered, holding me close to him and rubbing my hair. "If you are innocent my child, you have nothing to fear."

"I don't believe a word you're saying," my mother chimed in. "You have brought dishonor to our family and now you want to play like you're the victim. With everything in me, I believe that her disappearance was done by your hands and your hands alone. And when the Gods figure out that you orchestrated this whole thing, you are going to be sentenced to something far worse than death."

My father released his grip on me and walked over to my mother. He looked at her and then raised his hand to the Heavens and brought it down across her face with the strength of the Almighty behind his blow. My mother went sailing into the wall and then her body fell onto the floor. At that moment, my father stood over her and began to scold her like a child.

"Cherish, you will never speak ill of our daughter again. Even when she's wrong, she is right. As a family, we stand strong and support each other. And if by chance she is lying, know that what she has done, she has learned it from you. Now, you have two choices. One, you can run your mouth about what you think you know, and I will kill you. Or, you can choose option two and get up, shut up, and stand behind what our daughter has told us. You are not the Almighty and you have no right to judge," he huffed.

My mother didn't say another word. With tears running down her eyes, she got up from the floor quietly and made her way to the bathroom. My father then turned his attention back to me and demanded that I go back to solitary confinement and stick to whatever story I had told them.

He gave me a kiss on my forehead and told me that he loved me. With that being said, I made my way back to my prison through the storm and found comfort in my bed. If the Gods didn't kill me first, the quietness would.

~~~~~~~~~~~~~~~~~~~~~

Chapter Six

Ashley

My life was spiraling out of control. I couldn't think about anything except a hard dick being shoved deep within me. With all the testosterone of the males in this pack heightened because now they were able to procreate with the lionesses, it was hard for me to stay focused.

It didn't help that I could hear their thoughts and feel as they engaged sexually with each other. This made my clit throb constantly. I had even shifted into my cat a coupled of times and backed my ass up to the wooden postal on my bed and vigorously rubbed up against it. That scratched the itch but did nothing for my hunger for affection.

We it became unbearable, I remembered that as a teenage girl when I was first learning about sexual gratification, allowing warm water to dribble across your clit would give you one of the best orgasms in the world. My only problem here was there were no modern facilities…meaning these people didn't have bathrooms, they had bathing holes and ancient toiletries.

"You have the power…use it," I heard a voice say. I looked around my room and found that I was still the only person in here. Bullet had taken Serenity with him when they decided to lock me in my room. We all felt that it would be best for me to be in a secure location. They could come into my chamber, but I could not get out.

"It's inside of you. It's all around you. Think it and it shall be done," the voice said.

I got up from my bed and began to look around the room. Either someone was playing a hideous joke on me or I was going crazy. I looked in Serenity's room and found no one, I looked in the room where the hot springs leaked in for my bath…and I found no one. I even looked under my bed hoping that I would find a speaker or something because I didn't want to face the fact that I may be going crazy. Hell, I was already dealing with a complicated pregnancy, a needy pride, and my hormones raging out of control. Now, I have to face the fact that this solitary confinement shit was messing with my psyche.

"I'm not in your daughter's room, in your bathroom, or under your bed. I am who I am. I am the

Alpha and the Omega, the beginning and the end. I am he."

I fell to my knees and was overcome with a sense of tranquility. All my worries were washed away and even my sexual desires faded away like the setting sun. I was overwhelmed by the heavy odor of sweet spices: cinnamon, peppermint, ginger, and rosemary. I'm sure there were many others, but I couldn't tell you what they were. But I could tell you I was listening to the divine voice of the Almighty.

"My Lord," I said, bowing my head.

"What you seek is deep within you. Ashley, I blessed you with the best of my essence. Use you powers wisely and become a queen like no other queen. Stand strong, listen, and rule with your heart. Spread happiness and love, and in return, Alexandria will thrive like it once did during the time of your ancestors. The power is in you. Its all around you," the voice said softly.

After he finished that last sentence, I felt the divine energy dissipate. I stood up and several lightning bolts struck me. My body jolted violently with each one. It did not hurt but I could see the world more clearly. Everything began to make sense and my destiny was clear.

Hearing the noise, Bullet came rushing through the door. I could see the panic on his face and hear as his heart beat like a war drum. I looked at him and studied his being. He and Gethambe were only a small fraction of what I needed to accomplish. Serenity was the true strength and the one who needed my protection until she became of age. Although I was going to unite the two tribes, Serenity was going to be the wisdom Behind us leading the people into a brighter direction. Her words would become lethal and her faith to the tradition of the two tribes will be the strength. I saw as my daughter led our people into a battle that united all the prides and packs as one.

"Are you okay?" Bullet asked me.

Bullet was tall with a muscular physique, his smile was deep but sincere, and his heart was full of want and love for me. I could see that now. It was clear that we were meant to be. "Become my second husband," I said, looking my eyes on his.

"Your eyes are a soothing shade of green," he said

to me.

I walked over to him and wrapped my arms around his neck and pulled his bottom lip into my mouth. As he wrapped his arms around my waist, I began to suck on his bottom lip gently.

"You are mated to Gethambe and pregnant with his child. Being the gentleman that I am, I cannot enter your body. Although it would be the ultimate payback for everything he has done to me and our people, I can't," he whispered.

"There other ways to satisfy your queen," I said to him, now inserting my tongue into his mouth.

"Gethambe is on his way. He should be arriving any minute now."

"Be my number two," I said.

"What is up with your eyes, Mon Cheri?"

"My body is in need of a man," I answered, feeling my clit thump with want.

"I would love to be your husband, but I would only settle for the number one position," he answered, raining kisses down my neck.

"The number one husband needs to be aggressive; a military man. A husband with an attitude that has the loyalty of his army. You are not that person. Bullet, you are a number two," I whispered, enjoying as his tongue slid passionately up and down my neck.

"I'm not a weak man."

"The thought never crossed my mind. But we both know that Gethambe is the warrior and you are the lover. Know your place and settle into it," I moaned.

Bullet pulled away from me and looked at me surprisingly. I could tell that I was hurting his ego, but I saw our future together and it wasn't a bright one. Although I fell in love with him, his death was on the horizon. I watched as his body lay motionless on the steps of the temple. I saw as he was carried to the royal boat and was pushed out to sea. Serenity's tears bought about a great thunderstorm as the archer shot the burning arrow into the sky. As it hit its mark, Bullet's royal boat burst into flames and I could see his soul as it left its vessel and ascended into the Heavens. Gethambe stood at my side as we honored him with a Viking King's burial. A tradition honored by this pack.

"Do you not see the strength in me?"

"You have heart. And that is what is going to keep me grounded. I need you to balance me," I explained.

"But I would never be your first husband? After all I had to go through to bring you here and get you prepared for the role that you are about to take on…you still chose him?"

"He will always be the missing link. Without Gethambe, my heart would cease to beat. I need him to complete me. But I need you too. It's going to take both of you to work together in harmony to keep my beast and my succubus satisfied," I explained.

As he continued to look at me, a familiar scent invaded my nostrils. My body filled with excitement as I recognized the smell to be that of my husband. I pushed past Bullet and made my way out to the throne room where my husband was waiting for me.

I ran to him and jumped into his arms. He spun me around in circles as he kissed me passionately. Tears streamed down my face as tears swelled in his eyes. When he stopped and lowered me to the ground, his eyes widened as he gazed upon my stomach.

When he placed his hand on my stomach, it ignited a yearning in me that only he could satisfy.

"Where is Serenity?" he questioned, watching Bullet, who was walking from my bedroom.

"With the elders," Bullet answered.

I could see the anger in Gethambe as he heard Bullet's voice.

"What the fuck?" he yelled. "Ashley are you fucking this nigga while my seed is growing in your womb?"

"No. Bullet has been nothing more than a gentleman. Although I have taunted him and tested his patience, he respected you too much to take me in that way," I answered.

"Meaning...I could have fucked her, but I chose not to," Bullet chimed in.

Gethambe looked at Bullet with pure disgust and then began walking in his direction. When he was standing directly in front of him he asked, "What did you say, nigga?"

"I could have been knee deep in her pussy, spanking your seed's ass," he chuckled.

Without warning, Gethambe swung and planted his fist in Bullet's jaw. Bullet's body was flung backwards, slamming hard against the wall. When he was able to regain his balance, he wiped the blood from his mouth and replied, "It's on now, bitch."

He shifted into his lion and stood brave and strong. Bullet's cat was a gorgeous tawny brown with an eggshell white strip underneath him. His eyes looked at if he were a mystic grey lined with a black liner. Bullet's fangs hung from his mouth and his cat was muscular, carved to perfection. He was not only stunning in his cat form, but he looked fierce.

Not willing to be bitched out by Bullet, Gethambe wasted no time morphing into his beast. He was just a little bigger than Bullet and his rage game was strong. His coat was snow white, his eyes were a shamrock green, and his teeth were long and pointed. Gethambe's demeanor reeked that of a well-trained killer. He was emotionless and focused on his arch enemy.

When I turned to see all who were in the temple, I noticed that everyone was in their battle cat or savage wolf. I was the only person who was still in human form. Gethambe and the Canine Crew against an army of mountain lions; my heart told me that this wasn't going to end well.

As Gethambe lunged toward Bullet, I screamed. All I could do is think about the vision of Bullet's body laying bloody on the temple steps. He wasn't responsible for me being here, Lana was. Bullet had been nothing but kind and considerate of my needs and feelings. I couldn't allow Gethambe to take his life from this world. He was a part of me.

"No!" I yelled, trying to stop the inevitable.

Gethambe had made first impact with Bullet while the Canine Crew began to fend off the other members of the mountain lion's pack. Although Gethambe made a long slash into Bullet's right side; Bullet was able to attack Gethambe, using his claws to cut through Gethambe's body.

With both injured from the impact of the other's claws and teeth, they began to walk around in a circle, snarling and locking eyes. Gethambe was researching his opponent and Bullet was exploring Gethambe's behavior.

Although there were many more mountain lions than there were wolves, the Canine Crew were better fighters and held them back with ease. They worked together and moved as one, making the mountain lions, who were naïve to fighting, easy to fend off and keep from interfering with Gethambe and Bullet.

Gethambe began to increase his speed and changing his direction sporadically to confuse Bullet. Not knowing what to do, Bullet stood motionless and tried to analyze what was happening. When Gethambe noticed that Bullet appeared confused, he raced in and tackled him. They tumbled around the room, biting and pulling at the other. Blood was spilling from Bullet's body like a waterfall. He was growling out in pain as Gethambe ripped patches of hair from his body and used his nails to cut deep into his skin. During Gethambe's savage attack, it was apparent that Bullet was no match for him.

As my heart began to shatter, the room started to tremor. When the tears swelled in my eyes, my soul awakened. I could feel my body fall into a deep trance, overcome by a harmonic sensation. I could feel my body levitate from the floor, I could feel the wind blow ferociously through my hair, and I could feel the power of the Almighty wash throughout my body. I sat down on the air and crossed my legs, pulled my hands in front of me and placed them into a praying position. I cleared my mind, closed my eyes and began to softly chant repeatedly;

Caring, loving, and compassionate.

Understanding, warm, and sympathetic.

Kindhearted, tender, and charitable.

Lenient, loving, and bountiful.

Noble, generous, and patient.

Accommodating, concerned, and unselfish.

Humanitarian, merciful, and gracious.

Gentle, liberal, and chivalrous.

Thoughtful, polite, and attentive.

Considerate, helpful, and benevolent.

Each time I recited those words, one after another,

a member of each tribe sat quietly. They remained in their beast, but all their attention was focused on me. The last two to fall under my euphonious prayer were Gethambe and Bullet.

As the room quieted and the fighting ceased, I opened my eyes and looked at my people with love and forgiveness. I wasn't mad that Gethambe was jealous or that Bullet was trying to show his dominance. I just wanted us all to inhabit both realms in peace. They had been fighting for so long that they didn't realize that they were fighting their ancestors' battles. Neither side wanted to admit their fault and neither side wanted to forgive the events history had cursed on them.

"I love you Gethambe. I love you with all my heart. But you must control your jealousy, or it is going to get you killed," I said in a soft and loving tone.

Then I looked at Bullet and explained, "I love you too. Not as much as I love Gethambe, but your kindness has smitten my heart. You will be my second husband and rule this land as a first husband. Gethambe will be my first husband and rule the earthbound land as my first husband."

As I saw the look of disbelief on the other faces I stated, "There will be no more fighting between the wolves and lions. We are going to be a family and rule as one. Anyone who opposes me is encouraged to leave. Because if you stay, I will kill you myself. I have no room in my heart for hatred."

One by one they morphed into their human and bowed. As Gethambe and Bullet morphed, I could still see the hatred in both of their eyes. I lowered my body and stood on my feet. Gracefully I walked past Gethambe and over to Bullet. He was badly wounded from the fight, so I placed my hand on each wound and healed it. For each wound that I healed, my necklace illuminated with a bright white light.

"Alexandria is healing you. It's giving you a piece of her in return for peace, love, and understanding. Accept you position and help me lead our people back into the good graces of the Almighty."

"Do you realize what you are asking of me?" he questioned.

"My heart is fated to Gethambe, and my life to you.

You do not want me to choose a side. Your people wouldn't like my decision...and neither would you," I whispered.

"I told you in the beginning that I'm not sharing you with anyone," Gethambe snapped.

"Then leave," I said as I healed the last wound on Bullet. "I'm offering you my heart. I'm carrying your son. And I'm uniting two tribes. But if me sleeping with another man is such a burden for you, then leave. I'm not asking for you to give me anything that I haven't given you."

"This is not the way of our people," Gethambe said; his tone was harsh.

"Many moons ago, Queen Sheba was gifted two husbands. Although she was supposed to marry within her pack, like me, she gave her heart to the wolf. It was forbidden then for the blood to mingle, but since I am a half-breed, that doesn't apply to me. And, when Serenity reaches an appropriate age to marry, it won't apply to her either...because she drank from me, Serenity has the blood of a god. But the choice is yours, Gethambe."

He ran up to me and wrapped his hands around my throat. Before Bullet was able to come to my defense, I laughed. Little did he know, that shit was turning me the fuck on.

"Why are you doing this to me?" he yelled. "I love you and you're stabbing me in my chest,"

With my feet an inch or so off the ground I answered, "Fuck me."

Gethambe lowered my body to the ground and pulled me in for a long and sensual kiss.

~~~~~~~~~~~~~~~~~

Chapter Seven

Bullet

Since Gethambe and his elite friends of professional killers have arrived, he has dominated his role as the first husband and king. Because Ashley is pregnant with his seed, he gets the pleasure of sleeping in her chambers and making love to her every night. Although I get to spend time with her, it's not like the quality time that is shared between her and Gethambe.

"Bullet," Gethambe called out to me as he walked from Ashley's chambers. I was light weight pissed off as he approached me, displaying that arrogant grin and reeking of Ashley's cream. Nasty motherfucker didn't wash his dick on purpose. This was his way of taunting me.

"What?" I huffed.

"Rouge wants you to get your soldiers together. We want to start training them, Canine style," he laughed.

"Really?" I asked nonchalantly.

"I was thinking about calling them The Pussycats. What do you think?" he grinned.

"That's like calling the Canine Crew, puppy power," I answered. Little did this arrogant motherfucker know, we were the protectors. Our females hunted for them and watched over their lands. It was because of our people that they were not killed off. This stupid son-of-a-bitch probably had no clue about his arch enemy who is one of my people's distant relatives.

"Look, since we're brother-husbands, we might as well get along. As a matter of fact, to show you how much I care, I'll let you smell Ashley's cum on my dick." Then his arrogant ass pulled it out for all to see. Using his hips, he swung his dick from side to side, forcing the aroma of Ashley's cream to fill the air.

"Blue balls?" Rouge asked as he laughed hysterically.

"Gotta have balls for them to be blue," Joker joined in.

Ignoring their childish jokes, I redirected the conversation toward a name for our security team, "All jokes aside, I would like for you to refer to them as, The Pride."

Gethambe stopped swinging his dick and looked at me seriously and said, "The Pride?"

"That is what we are. Taking a title like that would symbolize unity and family. And the others that are not lion will be treated as equal. If you haven't noticed, we are a mixed family." When there wasn't many of us, we allowed members of other cats and some wolves to join our pack. They needed us just as much as we needed them.

"The Pride it is. Where do the males usually practice?" Rouge asked.

I looked at him in surprise. They really needed a history lesson. "Our males do train, but it was our women who do most of the fighting. Our females have always been the protectors of this realm," I explained.

They all looked at me with blank stares. They have women in their armies but it's their men who lead them into battle. Alexandria's strength is driven from the women who nourish it. Their spirits are rooted deep in the land. And when mother land is in need of protection, her daughters fight to keep her safe.

They are intelligent creatures with a lack of remorse. They are focused, disciplined and understand the importance of working together as one. When engaged in a battle, these women become true warriors and deadly animals.

"You want me to train a bunch of bitches?" Rouge asked.

"Things are different here, my nigga," Juice stated, spitting out a piece of meat.

"For sure," Stewart agreed. "I didn't sign up for all this crazy shit."

"I don't mind being around pussy all day," Joker laughed.

Ashley walked out of her chamber; she was looking to spend some time with Serenity. She had everyone's attention as she sashayed toward us. With her stomach now poking out, her hips widened, and her face glowing, she was angelic. I was captivated by her beauty and her innocent demeanor. The only downfall is that I could smell Gethambe all over her.

She walked over to me and wrapped her arms around my neck and smiled. "Did you miss me last night?"

"I miss you every night, Mon Cheri," I answered. I pulled her close to me and gently kissed her lips. Since we married, I could only cuddle with her. We were not permitted to become intimate until after she has given birth. But I could tell that Gethambe was keeping her succubus well fucked because every time she was around me, her eyes were the perfect shade of lavender.

She kissed me again and then made her way to Gethambe's right side. He looked in my direction and shot me a devious smile. He told me about the eye color change to torture me. It was only when her eyes were blue that she was in need of some sexual attention. But if they were lavender, her succubus was well controlled, and all her sexual desires have been fed. I believe it made that nigga's dick hard knowing that he was making me jealous.

But when it all boils down, I'm going to get the last laugh. As soon as I'm able to lay down my law and imprint on Ashley, I'm going to open her up like a Christmas present. I saw his dick and I believe I'm carrying more weight.

"I will be casting a spell to open the portal for the elders. Since the birth of Sheba, they have been blinded to this magnificent place, and I would like for my ancestor to see and appreciate this place as much as I do," she giggled.

"With all due respect, Mon Cheri, this place was hidden from her for a reason. She turned her back on her first husband and slept with another man while she was still married to Adam."

"I married Gethambe and now I'm married to you. Isn't that the same? And the Almighty hasn't cursed my womb or given me a sign that he doesn't want them to visit Alexandria. Didn't you tell me yourself that Sheba was raise by angels?" she questioned.

"Angels often roamed these lands...that much is true. But the elders have never seen this place because our land is holy. Although they live in Edom, and they are

106

considered angels – they are still partially demons," I explained.

Then her skin turned as white as snow along with her eyes. She looked up to the Heavens and spoke in Aramaic. This had to be a gift from the Almighty because that was the language of the Almighty himself. Only certain angels, Demi-Gods, and some humans that the Almighty used to deliver messages could speak the language. And no one left living here, not even myself, could understand it.

When her skin returned to its normal color and her eyes turned to a soft lavender she advised, "They will travel safely through the Portal of Life and they will be bringing Lana with them. She will stand trial here for her crimes against Serenity and me. She will be judged by a panel of lionesses and if death is her judgement, her blood must not spill here. She is to be taken to the Arizona desert and burned alive. As her spirit ascends from her body, it is to be given to Eisheth Zenunim, the soul eater."

Stunned by all the changes that were about to take place, I took a seat on the steps of the temple. The last time our people had contact with any sort of god, angel, or demon, we were being stripped of our privileges. Now that Ashley has returned, our lands are fertile, we have pups, and now we will be blessed with a visit from the elders. Although I have heard stories of them and had the pleasure of seeing them once while I was a cub, I was overcome with joy. That's until Gethambe opened his mouth and began talking.

"Ashley, you are the queen of two realms. Why do you dress like a peasant? I'm used to you wearing the finer clothing and smelling like cherry blossoms, but since you have been here, you reek of homemade soaps and cheap perfume."

"Gethambe," she whined. "Stop being mean," she smiled at him, igniting my anger.

"Don't let him get to you," she whispered.

"I cannot help it, Mon Cheri. He has a way of making me jealous of your relationship with him," I explained, as I watched him caress her body and shove his tongue into her mouth.

"Your time will come. These babies will be here

soon. I was showed a vision that I will give him three sons before the next full moon."

I thought about what she was saying and realized that the next full moon was only a couple of days away. She didn't look big enough to carry three pups...or will they be human-like?

"While Bullet is helping them train the ladies for battle, why don't you shimmer us back to our realm where I can take you on a shopping spree?" I heard Gethambe say to Ashley. "Besides, our babies are going to need the proper necessities to come into this world, especially if we have to bring them here from time to time."

"Serenity turned out fine," I snapped.

"Did she have a choice?" he asked in a threatening voice.

"Blame that other bitch you married. She was the one who placed a bounty on Ashley's head," I told him.

"What?" he asked.

"Oooo, you didn't know, Papa Smurf," I chuckled. "You mean to tell me that the man who sees all and knows all didn't have a clue that he was sleeping with the enemy?"

"How do you know this?" he released Ashley from his grip and walked towards me with his chest poked out.

"Because she solicited GG for the job," I answered.

"Lies!" he yelled. "Ashley was of no threat to her. Why would she want her out of the picture?"

"Watch your tongue, Thunder Cat, because the woman that you speak of is my sister," Rouge stated.

I didn't answer Rouge; instead, I sent for GG and her crew. They knew how they got into Achaemenid and she could tell them the details of their agreement. I didn't have the time or patience to sit here and listen to all the insults and be accused of being called a liar.

When GG and her crew arrived at the temple, I looked at her and insisted that she tell them everything that she remembered about that night.

"What are you talking about?" she questioned, looking at me in confusion.

"Tell Gethambe what you told me about Lana asking you to help her get rid of Ashley and Serenity," I pushed.

"I'm sorry Bullet. I don't think I know what you're talking about?" she answered.

I looked at her in amazement, trying to figure out why she was scared to talk about the incident in front of Gethambe and his crew.

"Nothing is going to happen to you. It's okay for you to speak your truth. Tell him how Lana came to the restaurant and asked you to rid her life of Serenity and Ashley," I begged.

"Are you sure that is what I told you? Could it have been one of the other members in the restaurant and maybe you're getting a little confused?" she asked.

"What the fuck is going on. Snoop? Rango? Moon?"

They all looked at me with a blank stare as if this was the first time they have heard this story. I knew then something wasn't right. My gut feeling said that somehow, someway, someone had mentally fucked my crew. Somebody here wasn't being honest, and my heart told me that Gethambe was behind it.

"I think your girlfriend has dementia," Gethambe

laughed.

"I know what she told me and that is how Ashley ended up here. As a matter of fact, ask Fatima. For some reason she still has a little respect bottled up inside of her for your people. She will tell you what she knows," I growled.

"Send for Fatima," Ashley intervened. *"I believe you,"* she whispered in my head. *"My memory is kind of foggy, but I feel like she had something to do with this too."*

"I have no reason to lie to you. Not even if I was promised your heart in exchange. I believe that you deserve to know the truth."

"How could she have gotten to them?" she wondered.

"That, I could not tell you. If she is being held in solitary confinement in Edom, she is confined by old magic. Besides, I don't think Lana is smart or powerful enough to cast a spell. She would have needed some help for that?" I responded.

"Rouge?"

"He's smart as far as military training and

execution, but he does not have the power she would need to accomplish this. I don't sense that in him. Plus, his loyalty isn't with his sister, his bond is secure with Gethambe."

"Juice, Stewart, or Joker?"

"I don't believe so. Let me think on it for a while. Here comes Fatima, lets see what she remembers."

"You sent for me, My Lady?" Fatima asked.

"What do you know about my kidnapping?" Ashley questioned.

"Only what GG has told me and a couple of other people, My Lady," she answered.

"And tell the Almighty Gethambe the story that was told to you," I said, looking in his direction.

"I was told that she appeared to them on the night of your wedding. That she led them to a cavern that was connected to Achaemenid. Lana led them into Ashley's chamber and allowed them to take possession of her and the baby. I believe she preferred them to be killed, but I may have not heard GG correctly," she explained.

"Then why do you lie, GG?" Gethambe's voice

became loud and irritable.

"I honestly don't remember telling such a tale," GG answered.

As Gethambe elevated his voice and demanded to know more, GG's lion tried to emerge. I could tell that it was taking all the strength that she had in her body to hold her lion at bay.

"I want this pussy's head on a platter," Gethambe demanded. "How dare she lie to a king."

I grew tired of the constant insults to me and my people. I was trying desperately to get along and make this thing work, but Gethambe was pushing my buttons.

I stood tall and strong. I faced Gethambe and his merry band of idiots and yelled, "I am Bullet James. I am the son of Abrey James, the once ruthless king that ruled these lands. I am a leader, a son, a husband, and a person. The many people that you have met within our city are not beneath you, here we are a family and don't place much value on titles. We don't measure our worth in the amount of money in our bank account, we measure it in respect. You don't have to stay here, you are free to leave whenever you like. And if Ashley wants to go to live out her years with an arrogant prick such as yourself, she too is free to leave. Our lands will sustain our people for a couple of years and this time we will make better choices. But I will not…cannot allow you to stand on our holy grounds and allow you to continuously degrade my people. That is not how we do things here, Gethambe!"

"Did I hit a nerve?" he laughed, stepping down the temple steps.

"You hit a nerve the day your mother spit you from her womb," I snapped.

"Round two of me kicking your ass?" he said as his Canine Crew all began to transform into their beast. All of them were salivating as they exposed their fangs while growling.

"There will be no more fighting," Ashley stated. "We are family…regardless of the tribe that we are from."

"I've played this game long enough, Ashley. Stay in your place and know your role," Gethambe said to her as he continued to approach me.

"Gethambe, I'm not a killer but don't test me," she

snapped at him.

He stopped in his tracks and turned and looked at her as if she was beneath him. He took two steps back in her direction and stated, "Remember these words? I will love and cherish your being. I will be **submissive** but supportive. I will **listen** to you and **support your decisions**. You are my king, my life, and my joy," he recited. "I will give you the **breath** from my body so that you can breathe. **Without you, there is no life on this world for me**. I give all of me to you. **Forever**," he finished.

"I remember," she answered quietly.

"A submissive wife you shall be," he snapped, turning his attention back to me.

He continued his descent toward me only to be stopped dead in his tracks. His body was unable to come any closer and the Canine Crew were immobilized. And as I began to search the crowd to find the source of this great power, my eyes fell upon this little body making its way towards me.

As Serenity emerged from the crowd, she spoke

only one word, "Silence."

She found her way to me and wrapped her arms around my leg and watched as her father stood there motionless. Ashley walked down the steps and over to where we stood, and she reached for Serenity who leaped into her arms.

I was dumbfounded to see that she had grown to a child around the age of six. She was beautiful but deadly.

"Be a good girl and release Daddy and his friends," Ashley told her.

"Mean," she told her mother.

"No, my little lotus flower. He's just upset that someone tried to hurt me and you," she smiled at her, using her finger to tap Serenity on her nose.

Serenity giggled as her mother played with her, then she wiggled her nose and freed Gethambe and his boys.

"What the fuck?" Gethambe said.

As the others morphed back into their human form, they too were astonished by the power Serenity possessed.

"Clothes," she said, and clothes appeared on their

bodies.

"Serenity?" Gethambe asked.

"Yes. She grows quickly here," Ashley answered, as she started back up the steps.

"Her skin color?" Gethambe questioned.

"She fed from me, so she will be like me," Ashley responded.

Gethambe followed Ashley up the steps and ordered the Canine Crew to begin training The Pride. I heard Ashley tell him that if he doesn't straighten up and accept that I was going to be a part of her life, that she would send him home and she would live out her years here, with me.

"I do love you," she whispered to me. *"Know that you hold a special place in my heart."*

"And I love you too, Mon Cheri. And although I hate to say it, I really feel like he does too," I confessed.

"After I put Serenity down, I will come and spend the night with you."

"But it isn't my night to have you," I said.

"I know, but I want to be in your arms tonight."

Chapter Eight

Gethambe

I am getting used to Bullet's ole bitch ass hanging around acting thirsty. I know that he couldn't wait to get his grubby paws on Ashley and it made my stomach turn knowing that after the babies are born, she would have to consummate her marriage to him. But until then, I'm going to continue to rock her world.

This morning Ashley woke up and her eyes were an amazing sapphire blue. I knew that she needed to feed, but it was becoming uncomfortable for her when we mated. She only wanted it one way and that was with her on top. If it was anyone else, I wouldn't mind it. But sometimes her succubus is a bit much to handle when she is in control.

"I want you," she said, her eyes glowing.

"I don't know if I want to give it to you. You side with Bullet and that pissed me off," I reminded her.

"Right is right and wrong is wrong. And in this case, he was in the right," she tried to defend her actions.

"I don't care if I'm wrong. You are to never speak

against me," I huffed.

"I understand," she answered.

"I don't care if you're the most powerful being in all the realms, I am your first husband and you will not disrespect me again. I need you to stay in your place and be the supportive, submissive wife you signed up to be."

"But this is my land, not yours," she stated.

"Correction. This is our land and we will run it as I run our affairs back home. And although I hate to say it, when I'm not here, you will respect and listen to Bullet. Since we are sharing you, it is your job as our wife to keep us both happy. Me more so than him," he laughed.

"So, I take it that you are beginning to accept this union?" she questioned.

"He's still a little bitch, but he's growing on me," I told her.

She sat up in the bed on her knees and cradled her stomach. I admired her strength and her drive for equality. She wanted everyone to get along all the time, regardless of her own happiness.

"Do you want to stay here?" I asked. I could tell

that she had fallen in love with her surroundings. She had become attached to the stress-free lifestyle that this place offered. And since I have been here, the livi-ng conditions had improved drastically.

Bullet and his people were doing a magnificent job rebuilding Alexandria. They had restored most of the building, repaired the paved roads, and began to grow their own food. They were truly a humble people. If nothing else I had to admire their devotion to making a change.

Rouge, Stewart, Juice, and Joker had begun to adapt to some of the ways of these people. Joker has even started to mate with a cute little jaguar that attached herself to him. They spend nearly every day together, and I'm happy to see him happy.

Rouge on the other hand seemed to be unsettled. I believe that although he doesn't want to admit it, he is concerned about his sister. They may not be close, but I'm sure he doesn't want her to be put to death.

"I want to be wherever you are," she answered, looking down onto her stomach. "I want my sons to grow up to be like their father. And if I'm here and you're there, you will miss important moments in their life."

"Then I guess you are going to have to split your time between Alexandria and Achaemenid."

She looked up at me with a growing desire for my hardness. Ashley reached over and grabbed it in her hand and began to gently run her hand up and down its length. It excited me to feel her soft hands glide up and back down it in a twisting motion.

"I need you," she stated. I looked at her eyes and noticed how the blue slowly changed to an emerald green. I couldn't understand why she needed it because I had just made love to her last night…twice. Her appetite for sex was increasing. I know that Lilith had warned me about these times, but I couldn't believe how it was happening so suddenly.

She leaned over and started to suck the precum that seeped out the tip. She roller her tongue around the head in circles, every now and then sucking gently on it. Falling quick for her to insert me into her mouth, I reached down and grabbed her by the back of her head and forced it downwards. Ashley had done this so many times before that she knew to relax her muscles and take it nice and slow.

As I pushed it all the way into her mouth, she allowed it to sit in the back of her throat for several seconds before pulling it out. Again, she took me into her mouth and began to bob her head to a slow love song that played softly in her own head. Ashley salivated on my hardness and used that for lubricant. I thrusted slowly into her mouth while she sucked passionately on my dick. Tightening her grip as she continued to massage it sent small waves of delight rushing throughout my body.

"Let me feel that tight pussy," I whispered.

She slurped up the remaining precum and sat up. She licked her lips and exhaled a seductive moan. I looked at her eyes and saw that they were still green, but I wasn't worried. I had some good dick and I was ready to lay it into her ass.

Ashley began to straddle me, but I didn't feel like a slow ride, I wanted to fuck. So, I pulled her onto my lap and flipped her onto her back. I pulled her left leg up onto my shoulder as I pushed inside of her with all my might. I immediately began to slam my hardness deep into her creamy center. I thrusted savagely with my balls smacking violently against her ass.

I could feel my dick swell inside of her and pulsate like a heartbeat. She moaned and dug her nails deep into my arms. I could feel her scoot backwards and that pushed me to an all new high.

I pulled out and flipped her onto her stomach and grabbed a fist full of her hair and pierced her core with one quick thrust. I wrapped her long hair around my hand and steadied myself by grabbing her hips and digging my claws into her. As I commenced to pound aggressively into her, she screamed out in exhilarating pleasure.

"Gethambe!"

"Who's your daddy, Bitch!" I yelled back at her.

"Fuck – Fuck – Fuck!" She cried out.

"Wrong answer," I huffed, now beating in her with quick, sharp, thrust.

"Who is your motherfucking daddy – Bitch!"

I could feel my blood warm, my heartbeat quickened, and the sweat pour from my body. I was working overtime delving deep into her soul and playing with her spirit. I was going to continue to punish this spicy minx until she yelled the answer that would satisfy my needs.

"I'm cumming," she panted.

So, I pulled out of her and pulled her up and dipped my head and sucked her cream from her body. It spilled freely for me and I became even more excited as her body jerked as her cum came rushing from her sweet spot.

When I drank all that she would give me, I spit on her pussy and pushed her ass back down onto the bed and shoved my full length back into her wetness. With my eyes half shut and my heart beating savagely against my chest, and my arms wrapped around her body, I pounded in her until I heard her yell out my name.

"Gethambe!"

"Who's your daddy?"

"Baby it's you," she cried.

"Wrong answer," I yelled, sucking hard on her neck and drilling my dick into her tight pussy.

She tried to crawl away to keep from cumming

again. Ashley knew better than to even test my gansta. Without realizing what I was doing, I had bit into her neck with my canines extended and stabilized her ass. Ashley had fucked up and released my beast.

Pound after pound, I slammed into her. With my claws extended, I slit the sheets and scratched up her body. She was moaning and screaming as I tortured her body in search of her next climax.

"Oh my god," she cried.

"No…It's Gethambe and god can't save you now," I growled.

I could feel my dick swell and my cum begging to be released. Her pussy was strangling my dick and her moans were pushing me so close to the edge.

I huffed, "Who is your daddy?"

"Gethambe! Gethambe!" She chanted.

Hearing her say my name sent a tsunami of pleasure racing through my body. Feeling her warm juices trickle from her core made my volcano erupt. With each spurt, my body bucked wildly until I had nothing left in me.

My breathing was heavy, and my body trembled whenever she moved beneath me. When I realized how I sliced her body and that we were laying in a puddle of blood, my heart began to race for a different reason. I knew I had killed the only woman I had ever truly loved.

I couldn't get up because I was still swollen inside of her, and she was laying there, not talking and not moving. I could tell that she was breathing, but her breaths were shallow.

"Ashley. Say something," I whispered in her ear, nibbling on its rim.

"My body aches," she whined.

"I know, Baby. I'm sorry. I've warned you about trying to run from me. It triggers the beast in me to catch the prey. As soon as I am able to pull out, I will go find a healer," I told her.

"I don't need a healer," she murmured.

"Baby, there's blood everywhere and deep cuts in your body. Unless you can heal yourself, I'm going to need to get you some help."

"My body is a part of Alexandria. I just need you

to carry me to the hot springs where I bathe and stay with me while the waters repair my body."

"Okay, Baby," I said to her. And I laid there with her until I was able to pull out of her body.

I took her to the hot springs inside of her chambers and stepped down into the water with her. I held Ashely close to me while I watched wound after wound heal. Then I grabbed the sponge and washed her body, removing all the blood.

"After the arrival of the elders, I will give birth to your children. This will be a time in my life that my body will be at its weakest. I will need the Canine Crew to guard my chamber with their lives."

"Baby, I won't let anything happen to you or my children," I assured her.

"Serenity must be in here with me and I will cast a protection spell over her room. Although she is strong enough to fend for herself, I don't want her to have to bear witness to any of the events that will take place tonight."

"Is it Lana? Are you afraid that she is going to do something to our children?"

"No. Tonight, we will face a bigger fear than Lana."

"What is it?" I questioned her, thinking that she was just hallucinating because of all the blood that she lost.

"Because these lands are rich and fertile, Abrey is going to return to try and reclaim these lands and me. And if he succeeds, he will kill our sons and daughter and place his claim on me. Because it is me, I cannot see my future. But I beg of you to protect Bullet with everything that you have in you. His father would kill him too in order to get to me. I am the key to his release," she explained as he began to drift off to sleep.

"Why tonight?" I questioned.

"The Portal of Life here opens to two realms, Edom and the Underworld. Normally they cannot pass through, but once every three thousand years the door that opens for us will open for them."

"Then don't open it."

She smiled at me and said, "We cannot run from destiny. And it is in our destiny to face off with Abrey and the Siberians."

"The Siberians? What the fuck is that, Ashley?"

"Your real nature enemy. They are known for killing your kind. That is why the lions were here for your protections. They don't want your money or land, they just want you to cease to exist."

"So, they will be here tonight?"

"Yes, My Love. If we survive this night, that is a battle we must prepare ourselves for. Like you, they are highly trained killers with a taste for wolf blood."

I helped her out of the tub and sat her in a chair beside the bed while I changed the bed for her. I assisted Ashley into the bed and covered her with a thick bison blanket. I leaned in and kissed her forehead. This was the first time in a long time that I saw her eyes turn back to their original color of hazel. They were soft, pure, and alluring.

"Get some rest," I whispered.

"Promise me you will watch out for Bullet when the times comes," she repeated.

I laughed and answered, "Although I don't like the little bitch boy, I will at least make sure that if anyone kills him, it will be me."

"You have a good heart, Gethambe," she said and snuggled deep into the blanket. Within a few seconds, she was sucking her thumb and sleeping like a newborn baby.

I made my way out of her chambers and into the throne room where I sat on the throne and became lost in thought. I haven't heard anything about Siberians or about them being our natural enemies. I needed to talk to my father and mother to see what they knew, but I had no way to open the portal and no one to guide them on the journey here.

"I just wanted you to know that you woke up half the pride with the little stunt you pulled," Bullet said walking into the throne room. "With all that I figured you both would be sleep by now."

"You seem to know a lot about our histories. What can you tell me about the Siberians?"

"Siberian Tigers?" he questioned.

"I guess. Ashley has been having a lot of visions lately, but not all of them come true."

"Well, if she is having visions about the Siberian

Tigers then you may want to go home and gather up your people before they arrive," he warned.

"Are they not safe in our compound?"

"Hell no," he laughed. I'm surprised they haven't come down here and wiped ya'll out before now."

"Why do they hate us?"

"Funny how wolves are supposed to be so smart and yet, you don't know anything. Before there were the wolves and lions, there were tigers. Now, although they are cats, they are lethal. Siberians don't mate outside their race normally, and the don't cohabitate with other tribes. In a way, they kind of remind me of you. They kill for sport and don't give a fuck about anyone but themselves," he joked, but I knew that Bullet meant every word he said.

"That doesn't say why they hate wolves so much," I snapped.

"Because you have what they want. To be honest, I have what they want. Sheba's successor."

"She was promised to them too? Damn, this chick comes with all sorts of baggage."

"They don't want her like we want her. They

would like to kill her. She is an abomination in their eyes. She is the living, walking proof that a cat and dog can create life. She is the only hybrid in the world that has a bloodline so tainted that they would kill to get rid of it. Ashley goes against their religious beliefs. And to be honest, so does Serenity," he explained.

"Another thing about Siberians, they will stop at nothing to get what they want. But the protection that is cast around the temple will protect us. This is holy ground and anything that isn't pure shouldn't be able to walk on these lands without the approval of the Almighty. Good thing for us is that they don't have a way to contact the almighty...unless they get their hands on someone like....Lana."

"Then we have nothing to worry about. I will send word home to my people to shut down the compound and make their way here. Together we will rule these lands in peace and harmony."

"Are you running from the fight?" Bullet asked.

"I fear no man or beast! But if I could spare the lives of those who are innocent, I will do whatever is in my power. You may see me as an asshole, but I generally care about those who are loyal to me."

"In that case, mi casa es su casa," Bullet smiled. "Now try to keep it down in there while I get a couple of hours of sleep."

"You don't have to worry about that. She is worn out and sleeping like a baby," I laughed.

He looked at me and cracked a half smile and made his way back to his chamber. I sat on the throne and continued to think about all the visions that Ashley was having and what was the meaning behind them all.

Then I thought about my people and flipped my switch to advise them to begin shutting down camp and I would send someone there to lead them back here. I told them that everything would be explained when they arrived.

~~~~~~~~~~~~~~~~~~~

Chapter Nine

Lana

I can see the tension between Samael and Lilith and I know that he can tell that I was the cause of her mistrust for him. Even the other wives have pulled away from him and sided with Lilith. Although they all loved him, they knew that he was a master of deception. Samael always told half truths and was excellent at persuading you to side with his views. But he has met his match because I am equally as devious.

Today we were traveling through the Portal of Life and I was as confident about facing Ashley as I am in my magic. She wasn't ready to face a real bitch. Where I spent many hours perfecting my craft, she toyed with her abilities. I have evolved into a new type of beast. I see life through new eyes and I keep my mind clear of my mischievous doings so that the pack can't intrude on my thoughts.

Lilith and her sister wives huddled in a corner and started to talk among themselves. I couldn't hear them, so I cannot say for sure if I was the topic of their conversation.

I really didn't care, because all of them were stuck in the dark times and couldn't tell their heads from their asses. The person that I was worried about was Samael. I know he could see that I escaped his magical prison and I know that he knows what I did to GG and her crew. But Samael observes and stays quiet, only striking when he goes in for the kill.

As Samael summoned the Portal of Life to open, he extended his hand and walked beside me. He glanced at me and smiled wickedly, and being the stone cold, heartless bitch that I am, I returned the gesture. This was a battle of the wits and I still had plenty of tricks up my sleeve.

Our bodies were pulled in and guided to our destination. When we emerged into Alexandria, I ran over to my sister wife and gave her a hug. I had to keep up the persona that we were fated to be together and that I truly missed her.

"You look ravishing," I smiled at Ashley. "Pregnancy really does showcase your beauty."

"Thank you," she replied, pulling away from me.

"Ashley," I gasped. "Have I offended you in some way?" I asked, placing my hand on my chest and pretending to be upset.

"Let's keep it real," she hissed. "You tried to dispose of me and my daughter and now you want to act like everything is cool between us. Lana…kick bricks and die bitch."

"Ashley?"

"I'm not stupid, Lana. I know that you were behind that whole little kidnapping thing. Just come clean and let Eisheth Zenunim suck your soul from your body. You don't deserve life," she snapped.

"I had no reason to harm you," I stated. I looked around the room to see that I held the attention of all who were present. I could see all the disbelief in their eyes, including those of my husband's.

Gethambe walked up to me and tried to analyze my spirit. I know that he couldn't gage my temperament or hear my darkest secrets because I cleansed my soul before arriving. All the wickedness that I had done up to this point was locked away and only I knew how to open the gates.

"Please tell me that you didn't do this, Lana," he said.

"I can say that all you want, but your essence has already judged me," I replied, backing away from him and lowering my head to the ground. If nothing else, I wasn't only a great liar, but I was an excellent actress.

Then the portal opened again and to my surprise, it was my mother and my father. They were here to bear witness to my trial. My father walked over to me and gave me a long, heartfelt bear hug, but my mother wouldn't even look in my direction.

"Now that we are all present, let's get this show on the road," Samael announced.

He led the way, followed closely by his wives. We walked through this elaborate temple with some of the most beautiful statues. As we walked down the steps, I was in awe of the beauty of Alexandria. It reminded me of Edom because of the serene atmosphere that enveloped you. I was surprised at how much life was here, because the last time I visited, it seemed to be a dying city.

As he led us through the paved roads, more and

more people came out to see the spectacle that was to take place. They waited patiently for us to walk past them and then they would join in the walk behind us.

When we reached the colosseum, I made my way to the witness stand and waited patiently for everyone to take a seat. As the placed filled, I showed no fear and even fixed my beautiful white gown that I had chosen for this occasion. It was long and silky, and hugged every curve on my body, only flaring out at the bottom. The sleeves were long and completely laced, and it was low cut in the front to give all a gracious view of my cleavage.

I looked my best and was prepared to walk away from this trial victorious. There was no proof and my dizzy ass sister wife's memory was impaired. The drugs that I used to knock her out had that affect, making one's eye witness account a little hazy.

When I finished messing with my gown and all were seated, I stood straight and waited for the trial to begin.

"State your name for the record," Samael announced; his voice was loud and thunderous.

"Lana Knight. I am the daughter of Pax and Cherish Knight and the rightful queen of Achaemenid," I answered; my voice was soft and kind.

"And how do you plead against the crimes that you are being charged with?" he questioned.

"Innocent," I replied. "Although no one has told me what I am being accused of."

"Kidnapping and attempting murder. You have two cases for each person involved."

"And who are the people that I have been accused of committing these crimes against?" I asked slyly.

He huffed, as if my line of questions were getting on his nerves. "Ashley and Serenity Knight," he answered.

"Thank you for that clarification," I responded.

Then he proceeded with, "It has come to our attention that you employed the help of GG and her crew to help you dispose of your sister wife and your only surviving child. Would you like to confess your sins?"

"The only sin that I have committed is not bonding with my daughter. I admit that I was upset that she was the only one to survive. A man needs a son to carry out his

140

legacy. And I will even go as far to admit that I was jealous of the relationship that my husband shared with Ashley, but with the advice of Samael, I accepted her into our life and sent my husband to go and get his bride. I have done no wrong here," I spoke loudly.

"Where were you the morning that Ashley was kidnapped?" he questioned.

"In my personal bath making love to my husband," I answered with ease.

"Liar!" he yelled.

"I have no reason to lie. He's right here staring at me as I give you this testimony. He can vouch for me and so can my brother who walked in on us as we were in the middle of mating." I knew that I had pinched a nerve with Ashley because he had just slept with her the night before. It felt so good digging the knife into her heart after all the fucking pain she has caused me.

"Young King?" he asked.

Gethambe stood up and stated, "Ashley was in her chamber while I was with Lana. We were engaged sexually, and her brother did walk in on us to give me the news that my second wife was not in her chambers."

"And while I was with my husband, he assured me that I would not have to worry about my position as first wife or Ashley's child becoming king. He promised me that if she had a son before we had one together, both first born sons would rule as equals. So, again, I had no reason to cause any harm to my sister wife. Neither my crown nor my child's position was challenged," I testified.

I could see as the wives became angry and looked at Samael for clarification. At that point I felt that the tides had swayed in my favor. The same exact story that I had told to Lilith, I repeated today for all to hear. Even Ashley looked a little unsettled learning that I may not have had anything to do with her kidnapping.

"Rouge, did you indeed see your sister with her husband the morning that Ashley was taken from the compound?"

Rouge stood up and looked at me with disgust. His loyalty was to Gethambe, not to me. He too knew my hands were dirty but had no proof. "Yes, My Lord. As my sister stated, I informed of Ashley's disappearance while he was dick deep into my sister," he answered.

Samael then turned his attention back to Gethambe. "Tell me young king, did you leave Ashley's chambers and go directly to Lana's?"

This sly motherfucker. I knew that he knew more than what he had let on. He was trying to back me into a corner.

"No. I made my rounds and checked on the people first. I had planned on going out to the city to go shopping for Ashley. I wanted her to feel like she was at home and I knew that she would need things for the baby," he answered, now looking at me suspiciously.

"And how long do you think it took you to make it to your first wife's chamber?" he questioned, now smiling at me wickedly.

Still, I stood strong and unfazed by his line of questioning.

"I would say that it took me about two hours," he answered.

"That surely seems like enough time for the foolish queen to do her dirty deed. Don't you think?" he asked

Gethambe.

Before he could answer I intervened. "My Lord, there is still one problem," I stated.

"And what might that be?" he asked.

"I had guards at my door from the time I was left alone with my children until the time my husband arrived. No one was allowed into my quarters and I was not allowed out. Gethambe was so angry with me for not bonding with his murderous daughter that he had them lock me in my room. I was treated like a common prisoner," I explained, allowing a few tears to stream down my face.

"Again. She is telling the truth. I did order her to be locked in her room. But when I thought about all the stress she had been under with losing her kids and accepting another woman into our marriage, I went to go see her. I did ask the guard if anyone had entered her chamber and he advised me that only the priest had been there to gather my sons for their burial."

Samael thought about it for a moment and closed his eyes as if he was having a vision. When he came back to, he looked at me and asked, "Is there another way out of your chamber?"

"None that I am aware of, My Lord. I have heard rumors of there being some, but no one has stated where they were," I answered, telling a partial truth.

"So, you don't know of *ANY* other way out of your chambers?" he questioned with an evil smirk on his face.

"My Lord, with all due respect, I feel that you are on a fishing expedition. Is it true that you knew where Sheba was all these years and you neglected to tell her mother?" I questioned him, now putting the spotlight on Samael.

"And what if I did?" he snarled.

"Then wouldn't it be beneficial to you to have Ashley disappear so that your dark secret would be safely hidden?" I questioned.

"Ashley had no knowledge of her ancestry trait, who Sheba was, or where Sheba was located. So, why did I have a need to rid her from Achaemenid?"

"I beg to differ. Slowly but surely Bullet was giving her more and more information about her past. Eventually she would have put two and two together and leaked the information to Lilith that you have deceived her for years about knowing the location of her offspring." Boom! There it is. I was overjoyed on the inside knowing that I had just fucked his whole case up against me.

I could see Samael begin to panic and noticed all the wives stand up and look in his direction for an answer. Even Ashley was now seeing things from my point of view. I was beating him at his own game and he knew it. I was quick with my answers and I made him look even more guilty than I.

I didn't even know for sure that he knew the location of Sheba. I just tossed the rope in his direction and waited patiently for him to hang himself. Now all I had to do was reel him in for the kill.

"Also, My Lord, I believe that I read somewhere in one of our history books that an Angel descended from the sky and opened the gates that held Sheba hostage. He knew that a spell had been cast over her and that nobody would be able to track her movements. By any chance My Lord, was that angel you?" I questioned.

By the looks on his face, I could tell that I had just

hit the hammer on the nail. Boom again...shots fired and angel down. Nothing he said would dig him out of this pile of shit. He was guilty, and I had just proven myself innocent.

All the times that they called me 'stupid queen', 'foolish queen', they had not taken the time to see that I was actually keeping track and taking names. I studied them intimately and learned all I needed to know about their past...with a little help from the enemy. I couldn't help but pat myself on my back. I wasn't the only one walking around with a dark cloud hanging over my head. I mean, I understand why he did what he did, but since he wanted to be an ass to me, I just let his secrets out in a not so nice way.

"Samael?" Lilith questioned, as she began to walk toward him. Her body looked worn and she looked at if she was emotionally drained. Lilith looked as if she had been hit by a train. In all honesty...I really felt sorry for her.

"I couldn't tell you," he stated.

"You mean to tell me that you really did know?"

she questioned.

"This is not the place to have this conversation," he snapped.

"You sorry son-of-a-bitch!" she yelled. "You knew where our daughter was, and you didn't tell me!" By this time all the sister wives were standing strong with her in disagreement about what he did. None of them could have children and they all felt Lilith's pain when her child was taken from her before she even had a chance to see her daughter.

"I did what I had to do to keep your mind straight. And I opened the gates and released her from this prison, so she didn't have to marry the mad king, Abrey. He would have killed her because of his lust for power," he explained.

"And you didn't tell me?" she questioned.

"If I would have told you about our daughter, she too would have died. Then there would be no descendants of our bloodline. You were cursed, My Heart. For the crime you committed against the Almighty, you were not to bear any children. And when one seed slipped through and became fertilized, I promised him that if he gave her life, I would keep the secret about her whereabouts," he said to her, pulling Lilith into his arms.

"How did she die? She was supposed to be immortal," she cried.

"She knew that once she abandoned Alexandria, she would be forfeiting her immortality. But Noel made her happy and she wanted to sacrifice herself to spend happier years with him. I promise you, My Heart...I watched over her with hawk eyes and made sure she lived well."

"I'm sorry I had to bring all this to light," I said sympathetically. "But I needed to show you that I had no reason to harm Ashley or Serenity. I would have gained nothing and as you can see, I would have lost everything."

"Lilith, Gethambe, Ashley...what is your take on her case?" Samael asked.

"Innocent." Ashley was the first to answer.

"Innocent." Gethambe stated, as he began to walk toward me.

"Innocent." Lilith answered, still emotionally

unstable from all that she had just learned.

I took a big sigh of relief because I had just escaped a death sentence. That was until I heard a little voice say. "Guilty."

When I searched the crowd to see who it was, there stood a young girl. I had no idea who she was or why she would speak up at my trial.

"Why do you say that, Serenity?" Ashley asked her.

"Because I can see the truth," she answered.

"How could this be? There is no way that monster could be my child. She's black," I blurted out.

~~~~~~~~~~~~~~~~~~~~

Chapter Ten

Ashley

As I lay in this bed in labor, I'm terrified. Everyone dismissed what Serenity said about Lana, thinking that she was just a baby when this happened, and she couldn't have known about her kidnapping. But she is not a regular child. She was born into immortality and fed from the breasts of a partial Demi-God...why would they even question it?

"Oh my god!" I cried out as another labor pain rocketed throughout my body. Hearing me cry out, Gethambe came bursting through the door to save me.

"Is she okay?" he asked.

"She's in labor young king," Lilith laughed. "This is not your first rodeo."

"I don't remember Lana yelling like this. She sounds like you're killing her in here," he said, his voice trembling.

"Calm yourself, Gethambe. Your children are fine," Na'amah tried to soothe him.

"I am calm," he stated. "What the fuck do you mean by calm yourself?" he asked, pacing the floor.

Lilith walked over to him and pulled him into her arms. "They are going to be fine," she whispered to him. "I can feel that you are worried about your babies, but I can assure you, they are going to be fine."

"Serenity!" I yelled. "I need Serenity to be in her room. These are dangerous times for her," I explained.

"Serenity is outside playing with the cubs," Na'amah said. "Why ruin her day and make her come in here where I'm sure you are going to scare her to death. A child doesn't need to be around all that screaming."

"You don't understand," I tried to warn them.

As I tried to breathe through the pain, Bullet walked in the room.

"Bullet! Go get Serenity and bring her to me!" I yelled, making him stop dead in his tracks.

"Is this a pregnancy thing, Mon Cheri?" he smiled.

"I had a vision. The Siberians are coming," I whispered to him.

"Mon Cheri, they cannot get past the gates. They are protected," he replied.

"Jesus! Hurry up and get them out of me!" I yelled.

"Don't you have some type of witch power to kill the pain?"

"Breathe," Eisheth Zenunim said.

"I'm about to kill this bitch," I said to Bullet causing him to laugh out loud.

"Get out of here with that foolishness," Agrat bat Mahlat snapped. "She needs a peaceful environment while she is giving birth.

"Please. I beg of you to go and get Serenity and take her to her room. It's protected with magic and they will not be able to get her," I pleaded.

"Never beg for anything, Mon Cheri. I will go get the little terrorist and put her down for a nap," he answered.

"We are not having any more children if I cannot have them in at human hospital!" I yelled a Gethambe.

"We don't know what the babies will come out looking like. We have to be careful," he said.

"Fuck being careful and give me something to ease this pain! Or get the fuck out of my face," I cried.

"She doesn't have much tolerance for pain. Even

Lana handled it better than your descendant," Na'amah giggled, talking to Lilith.

"Na'amah, be glad that you are Samael's wife," I warned. She just doesn't know how close she was to getting the business. She has never been pregnant and has no clue how much pain my body was in. At times I thought that the babies were trying to claw out of me.

Gethambe sat beside me and stroked my hair, trying to help calm my nerves. I could see that he was troubled, probably thinking about his children and hoping that nothing would happen. And I wish I could tell him otherwise, but I couldn't. Not that I thought that anything would happen to our children, but I kept having the re-occurring vision that Serenity and I were in trouble.

Then I also kept having the vision about Bullet and how I saw his body laid out on the temple steps. It was still, and his eyes were are open. I could see that he was laying in a puddle of blood and there was a long slit across his throat. I don't know what happened beforehand, but I keep seeing the Siberian Tigers invading these lands.

Bullet came into the room with Serenity and

brought her over to me so that I could kiss her before she laid down for a nap. She laid her hand on my stomach and laughed.

"What is so funny, Little Lady?" I asked her.

"Because there aren't three boys in there," she answered.

"And how do you know this?" Gethambe questioned.

"Because Zira said she wish ya'll would stop calling her a boy," she giggled.

"Zira?" Lilith asked.

"Yep. She said to tell you that she likes the name Zira," she laughed.

"So, you can communicate with them?" Gethambe asked.

"Yep. And my brothers said that the first one out gets the name Dion and the second one is stuck with the name Malik," she said. Her smile was so beautiful, and her giggle was so innocent.

"Serenity," I whispered to her. "Did they tell you when they were going to come out by any chance?"

She placed her little hand on my stomach and rubbed it gently. Then she looked at me and said, "Before the tigers arrive."

There was an unsettling quietness that fell over the room. We were all stunned by her revelation.

Gethambe picked her up and held Serenity in his arms. He kissed her on the forehead and said, "You don't have to worry about that my sweet little rosebud. This place is protected by magic and they can't get through the gates. We are perfectly safe here."

"We are safe as long as we stay in the temple. This is the source of Mommy's magic. Nothing can get through these walls and get us," she smiled.

He looked at Bullet and then at the wives. They were all thinking the same thing and that was to get the people inside the temple. We knew that they would be safe inside of here and we could hatch a plan to counter their attack.

"This child cannot know this," Lilith said.

"But she does, and we need to get the people inside of the temple," Bullet said, rushing out of the room.

"I feel pressure," I cried as tears began to stream down my face.

One of the wives grabbed Serenity and told Gethambe to help gather the people. As they dashed out the door, Serenity spoke again.

"Momma Lana doesn't need help. They already know her and that is why she removed the spell of protection on the gate."

My heart sank deep into my stomach when Serenity said those words. I knew that Lana couldn't be trusted, something inside of me said that she still harbored ill feelings because I was giving birth to Gethambe's children. Her hatred for me was so strong that she would side with anyone if they could dispose of me.

"Mommy don't worry. We are going to be okay."

"What about the people back home?" I questioned.

"Uncle Samael got them out," Serenity answered. She waved her hands and a hologram appeared. We could see as he helped the people of Achaemenid into the Portal of Life, guiding them to Edom.

"Ooooo," I yelled, feeling a pushing sensation

between my legs.

Serenity started to clap as Lilith and Na'amah helped Dion out of my womb and into this world.

"He has a human form," Lilith announced happily.

We could hear yelling outside the temple and loud thunderous noises. We could hear as the lioness roared as the prepared for battle. I could feel the ground shake as if we were experiencing an earthquake.

"I can feel another one," I yelled out.

Gethambe tried to take Serenity to her room, but I heard her when she told him, "Daddy, if you go out there, you will die. Today is not your day to be the hero."

It amazing how advanced she was. She talked in a cute little baby voice, but she carried a conversation like a grown woman. Her words were precise and her understanding of what was going on around her was deep. In human years, she was only a year old. But to see her, she looked about seven or eight. Although she wasn't tall, she was extremely intelligent and beyond her years.

As my second son made his grand entrance as Gethambe was taking Serenity to her room, she looked over at me and said, "Mommy, don't worry. You misinterpreted your vision. Daddy Bullet doesn't die. At least not today," she announced.

With tears streaming down my face, I thanked the gods for being so gracious. Not only were my children going to survive, but Bullet isn't going to leave me.

As they pulled Malik from my womb, I heard him cry. Although I hadn't laid my eyes on either of my sons, I was in love with them.

"And he looks human," Na'amah announced.

Before I could say anything, Zira was pushing her way out. Before any of the sister wives had a chance to care for Malik, Zira was already here. I guess she didn't want to wait any longer.

She was the first one that Lilith handed to me. As I cradled her in my arms, I showered her with kisses. She was a pleasant surprise for me. With the war raging outside, just holding her tiny body in my arms silenced my fears. I knew as long as we stayed a family, we would be untouchable.

"I believe they are all blind. They look like

humans, but they have the wolf trait," Na'amah explained.

"What makes you think that they are blind?" I asked, mesmerized by Zira's beauty.

"Because all of their eyes are cloudy. Those are not normal colors for a human or wolf," Na'amah answered.

As Zira moved her little head, I knew she could smell the milk and was searching for the nipple. So, I gently guided her head in the right direction and helped her to latch on.

We could still hear the war as it raged on. I was afraid for our friends and families that were out there fighting for their lives while we remained safe within the temple. I was a powerhouse that could move mountains but instead, my body decided to give birth.

I could have stopped this war and demolished Lana with a flicker of my hand. Instead, I was laying in this bed recovering. But I made a silent promise to myself that once my body was healed and these babies were no longer feeding from me, I was going after Lana.

"Do you hear that?" Gethambe asked.

"I don't hear anything," Eisheth Zenunim answered.

"Exactly my point," he replied. "I'm going to go and see what is going on. Close the door behind me as soon as I leave," he directed.

Gethambe handed Malik to one of the sister wives and slowly made his way out of the door with Lilith quick on his heels. As they left my room, Na'amah ran over to the door and closed it immediately. In reality, the only door that needed to be closed was the one leading to the outside. This temple sat on holy ground, the very place that the Almighty spilled his blood and blessed with a sacred prayer.

His prayer and blood were the strongest protection spell known to men and gods. If you had ill intentions of doing any harm to anyone, the temple would not allow you entrance. This was old blessed land that could not be destroyed or infiltrated by anyone that may have wanted to cause harm to me or my children.

When Gethambe and Lilith returned, I could see devastation on their faces.

"What is it?" I asked as my voice trembled with fear.

"Give the baby to Na'amah," he said. "I need you to see something."

She raced over to me and grabbed Zira from my arms. With the help of Gethambe and Lilith, I was able to get out of the bed. But I was too weak to walk, so Gethambe carried me in his arms.

As we walked through the throne room, our people bowed. I noticed that the Canine Crew were all accounted for, but they looked like that had been in a serious battle. Before we made our way to the door, I had Gethambe stop so that I could ask Rouge a few questions.

"Did your sister really open the gates for the Siberian Tigers?"

"I don't know," he answered. "Everything happened so quick. I remember her sitting by the waterfall, singing, but then there were a rush of large orange and black cats. They were quick and well trained. They knew what they wanted, and they knew these grounds like this was their home or like that had the blueprints. These are not your every day, run of the mill type of tigers. These huge motherfuckers are straight fucking killers."

"Did everyone make it inside?" I was really asking about Bullet, but I wanted them to know that I was equally concerned about the people.

"The lionesses knew their shit and protected everyone. They are fierce and disciplined soldiers. Without those ladies, we would have lost some lives today. We were able to get everyone into the temple with little or no injury. But I'm afraid that Bullet left out to shut the gates," he explained.

"He what?" Gethambe's voice was elevated.

"I tried to keep him in here Gethambe, but he wouldn't listen. I even told him that you ordered him to stay within the temple because of his royal obligation, and he still left. I'm sorry I failed you," he apologized.

"No need for apologies, brother. I know you did everything in your power. Your loyalty would never be something I would ever question," Gethambe assured him.

"And I would never question your loyalty either," I stated.

As we started toward the door, I could feel my heartbeat quickened with fear. If Bullet wasn't inside the temple with the people, I knew that he would be laying on the steps outside of the door.

"Put me down and let me stand on my own two feet," I said to him.

Without questioning me, he did what I asked and lowered me to the ground. It only took me a few seconds to pull myself together. As the doors opened, I realized that my vision was correct. There on the steps, by the door, laid Bullet in a puddle of blood.

I ran to his body and sat down in the puddle of blood beside him. Tears were pouring from my eyes because it was only then that I realized that half of me was missing. I pulled a part of him onto my lap and rocked swiftly back and forth.

As I cried, I remembered that I had the power to heal. I frantically started to look for the wound on his body that took his life. If I could heal it before Anubis arrived to take his soul, I could bring him back.

I extended my claw and slashed open his shirt.

Gethambe, realizing what I was searching for, joined me. Within a few seconds, we had him laying on the ground completely nude and I found two deep wounds. One was across his neck and the other on his inner thigh.

I placed one hand on each wound and allowed my energy to flow though him. As my hands glowed, I could feel as his blood warmed, and I could hear as it began to pump to and from his heart.

"Hurry, child. I hear him coming for Bullet," Lilith warned.

We could all hear the death drums beating loudly.

"Breathe," I whispered, "Breathe."

Lub – Dub, Lub – Dub, Lub – Dub, I heard. It was his heart and it had begun to beat. When he opened his eyes, my heart filled with joy. I leaned in to him and gave him a sweet and passionate kiss.

"Because you have escaped death, you owe me a life," Anubis stated as he stood over us.

"Not my children, Anubis," I cried out. "Take me," I pleaded.

"No. I offer my life for that of my king," I heard a

voice behind me say.

Fatima appeared in the door and started to make her way down the steps.

"What?" I sniffled.

"Bullet saved my life when I was shunned from my pack. For that, I owe him. I'm tired of all the fighting in this world and my body is ready to retire. I have been fighting for so many years that I don't know what it is like to rest. Anubis take my life for that of my king."

"I will see you next lifetime," Bullet told her. "Thank you."

She ran back to him and gave Bullet a kiss on his forehead. And then she turned to me and said, "Be good to him. He's a good man with a caring soul. He will love you, cherish you, and treat you like the queen that you are."

Then she turned to Anubis and said that she was ready. He hit his staph on the ground and a spiral portal opened for them. Instantly, they disappeared into the beautiful white light.

~~~~~~~~~~~~~~~~~~~

Chapter Eleven

Bullet

Once again, we are rebuilding our land after taking a devastating blow. I have been working with Gethambe to secure our borders to ensure this doesn't happen again. We all know that if the gates remain closed, no one can get in or out without the assistance of a gatekeeper.

Because we hadn't needed one, we never really worried about intruders. These lands were cursed and dead. Other species couldn't see the beauty of this place because it was overshadowed with death. But since the arrival of Ashley, the land is alive. It is filled with prairies of deep green grass, large oak trees, beautiful flowers, and a stream that brings fresh water for the people to drink.

We had decided that it would be best if the Canine Crew would man the gate and The Pack make surveillance runs around its perimeter. We both agreed that since they are highly skilled in stealth maneuvers, that they would be best suited prowling around the outer gates, looking for any sign of the Siberian Tigers. They didn't obtain what they were after, so we knew that they would return.

Gethambe and his crew have been generous with the money from their people. They have been bringing truckloads of furnishings, clothing, and food for everyone to enjoy. They even obtained some playground equipment for the cubs to play on. Since we are having more and more births, we needed to add some parks to keep the kiddo's happy.

Things are how they should be now. Ashley sits on the middle throne, Gethambe sits to her right, and I am on her left. Although this is my home, I agree that Gethambe should be her right hand. He is a lot more skilled in military procedures, was raised by a king and knew how to handle the daily kingdom duties and was arrogant and cold when he needed to be.

That life wasn't really my calling. I am more of the father figure type of guy. I enjoy spending my day with the kids and teaching their lessons. Although I'm not biologically their dad, they see me as their father and address me as such. Like Serenity, Zira and the boys are growing quickly. Serenity is now a teenager and the little ones are walking. They are only a couple of weeks old and they are freaking walking.

Now that Ashley's body has had some time to heal, we all agreed that tonight will be the perfect time to consummate our marriage. I had yet to experience the pleasure of my wife. My craving for her is strong and it grows stronger by the day. I'm scared in a way because I don't want to not be enough for her, but I don't want her to kill me either because I'm being too gentle. I've heard her and Gethambe get it on and I don't know if I can match his aggressive nature.

"Can I talk to you for a minute," I asked Gethambe.

"Sure," he answered. He looked at Rouge and told him that he would get back with him later. They were trying to locate Lana's whereabouts while trying to close all the hidden passages in Achaemenid. Although the two tribes have come together as one, we had made plans to still reside in two places. Gethambe's family still had businesses to run and they were trying to help our people to become financially independent as well.

"What's up?" he asked.

"Ashley."

"Something wrong with one of the children?"

"Are you deaf? I said Ashley," I repeated.

"What about Ashley?" he asked, as we started back to the temple.

"The sun is setting and tonight will be the first time that we are to mate," I blurted out.

Gethambe looked at me in confusion. "She's like any other woman. Just blow her fucking back out," he stated.

"Can I trust you with a secret?"

Gethambe stopped walking and turned to me. He now knew where this conversation was heading. "You mean to tell me that you're a virgin," he laughed.

"Ssshh," I tried to hush him.

"Nigga...for real?" he continued.

"I've seen others do it before, I just never had time to indulge. And when I was getting close to doing it, you would swoop in like a black Bat Man and steal the girls away," I tried to explain. Gethambe has been my rival for many years. Whenever I was interested in a female, he would show up and do that cocky shit and they would just melt in his arms. And it didn't help that I didn't have the financial backing that he had. Gethambe would splurge all night long on a piece of pussy that he was interested in banging.

"Look. You are just going to have to wing it. I can't teach you how to lay pipe to your wife. But, because I care about your wellbeing, I will be close by just in case you need some help. Her succubus game is strong," he chuckled, patting me on the shoulder and walking away.

I continued to mingle around the place until the sun began to set. As I made my way to the temple, I could hear Ashley talking to me.

"I'm in your chambers and I'm naked," she said.

"I'm close," I answered her.

"Hurry. I'm wet, excited, and I need to be fed," she whined.

I hurried up the temple steps and into the throne room where Ashley was waiting for me. She had morphed into her panther and she stood beside her throne and purred like a kitten. When I looked to the right, I saw Gethambe and his sidekicks watching as if we were about to give them a show.

This motherfucker told Joker, Juice, Stewart, and Rouge that I was a virgin and I had no clue on how to please my wife. And now they are all sitting back and waiting for the fireworks. I thought we were better than that.

"Gethambe?" Rouge called.

"What's up?" he answered, slicing an apple as he rested his body against the wall.

"What color are Ashley eyes?" he asked.

Immediately, Joker burst out into a hysterical laughter. Then I noticed that this very seductive black panther making her way towards me. Her body was sleek, her stride was elegant, and her purr was harmonizing.

Gethambe looked up and answered, "Green." Then he proceeded to insert a piece of the apple into his mouth.

"And what does green eyes mean?" Stewart questioned. I knew that he already knew the answer to the question. They were just trying to rattle my nerves…and it was working.

Gethambe laughed slightly and answered, "I

172

haven't fed her in a couple of days. She's hungry as fuck right now."

I looked at Ashley as she stood directly in front of me. Her purr was now vibrating my skeleton. As she sniffed me, her whiskers whisked pass my face sending delightful chills racing throughout my body.

"Is it safe for him to be with her right now?" Juice asked.

Gethambe looked up and smiled at me while winking his eye. "Nope. She's about to tear his naïve ass to pieces." His answer made all of them laugh. Then they proceeded to walk away, leaving me to fend for myself.

"You got any pointers…brother – husband?" I yelled out.

"Keep pushing until her eyes turn lavender," he answered, shutting the large double door behind them.

Ashley pulled me by my shirt and led me into my chambers. As I entered the room, she waved her paw, making the door close behind me. Her dark skin, long golden claws, and captivating green eyes had my cum already seeping out of my hardness.

I didn't have to remove my clothing because with one swipe of her paw, my entire outfit was laying on the floor in pieces. She looked down at my hardness to size me up and then back at me. As she shifted back into her human form, she grinned.

"I promise to take it easy on you," she said, walking toward the bed. She turned to me and allowed me to look at her gorgeous body. I have never gazed upon anything more beautiful. Her skin was smooth and a perfect shade of mocha, her frame was small, her breasts were full and her hips thick. As she sat on the bed and opened her legs wide for me, I slowly walked over to her and dropped to my knees.

I buried my head deep between her thighs and inhaled the sweet scent of her kitten. As I rubbed my nose around in it, she leaked a small amount of cream. I extended my tongue and flickered it across her tiny nub. I could hear her moan passionately.

Following her lead, I stuck one finger deep into her. Ashley grabbed the back of my neck and pulled me into her as she slowly rotated her hips, fucking my finger gently. I sucked, nibbled and bathed her lady fervently. She moaned softly and purred avidly.

Then she pushed me back and scooted backwards onto the bed. I noticed that her eyes were changing colors slowly. As I crawled into the bed and positioned my body between her thighs, they were a magnificent shade of sapphire blue. Her face was so angelic and welcoming that I couldn't help but to shower her with a million kisses.

As I ground against her body, I became too excited and shot my cum onto her stomach.

"Fuck," I whispered. "Isn't this fucking embarrassing?" Then I rolled over onto my back.

Ashley didn't let that stop her quest for her orgasm. She rubbed my cum into her body like lotion and sat up in the bed beside me. Her face was non-judgmental.

"Am I your first?" she questioned.

"I fingered a woman before and even gave you head once. I have just never experienced the actual act myself. I didn't have time," I explained.

"Well then. We have all night," she said. Then she lowered her head and inserted my soft meat into her mouth.

She pulled her hair around to the left side of her neck so that I could watch her as she sucked me.

Her mouth was extremely warm and cotton soft. As she bobbed her head up and down, she stroked my manhood until it grew to its fullest potential. But she didn't stop when it got hard…no, she kept sucking. Her stride was slow and tantalizing at first, but when it got hard, her stride became fast and savage

I thrusted my hips upward into her mouth, slamming it deep down her throat. The harder she sucked, the more excited I became. I could feel my balls tighten, my heart race a marathon, and my toes curl under like the witch in the Wizard of Oz.

"Fuck," I yelled out.

When she felt my hardness began to pulsate in her mouth, she stopped sucking and began to stroke it fast, gripping on to it for dear life. I couldn't help but to hold my breath as my nectar shot out of my body like the Old Faithful geyser. Ashley quickly inserted my hardness deep into her mouth, pushing it to the back of her throat. As my body jerked and my breath became caught in my throat, she sucked and swallowed all that spurted from my body.

Even after I had erupted, she continued to suck passionately on it. The tingling sensation made me rise to the occasion one more time. This time as my manhood hardened, she straddled me and slid her body down the length of my steel rod. She was soaking wet and extremely tight. Her wetness was strangling my hardness like Jack the Ripper.

Ashley swirled and bounced on my hardness like she was riding a bull in a rodeo. All I could do is push up into her forcefully and slam her down onto me viciously.

"Yes, Baby…just like that," she moaned.

Hearing her voice made me want to give her more. So, I flipped her over onto her back and began slamming into her core without mercy. As the euphoric feeling took over me, I pulled her legs up and jackhammered into her as my balls smacked her ass.

"Yes. Yes. Yes!" she yelled. "Fuck me hard and fast!"

Obliging her request, I continue to pound violently into her. My blood was now on fire and my desire for her cream was fueling my quest. I pulled out of her in mid stroke and pushed her legs all the way back, exposing her asshole. I kissed it before shoving my tongue into her ass and fucking it.

"What in the fuck are you doing to me?" she cried. Her juices now flowing from her body like a steady running river. Quickly, I made my way upward and sucked her dry before letting her legs down and flipping her over onto her stomach.

This time, I inserted myself into her slowly. I nibbled on her ear and licked her neck while I slowly stroked in her wetness. I pushed into her core and pulled out with precision. She buried her head deep in the pillow as her body surrendered its secrets to me. Her cream was gushing from her body and she could not stop shivering.

I wrapped my arms around her and continue to thrust in her core until I too exploded. As her body calmed, mine ignited with a series of wild jerks as I came crashing down into euphoria. My first time being intimate was amazing. I held her close to me until the last drop of my nectar poured into her body. At that very moment, Samael and Lilith shimmered into our bedroom.

"Move out of my way," Lilith demanded.

I rolled over and laid on my side as she smiled at Ashley. She was worn out from working me overtime. She rolled over and allowed Lilith to touch her stomach to see if she was with child. Unfortunately, I had not succeeded in impregnating my wife.

"Keep trying," Samael encouraged. "I thought she would surely be knocked up since you haven't had pussy since the day you slid out of one," he laughed.

"Does everyone know?"

"Gethambe made sure we all knew," Lilith laughed. "He thought he was going to have to come in here and save your life, boy!"

I looked at Ashley and noticed her eye color. "Well, for this being my first time, I had no problem making those beautiful babies turn purple."

"Well done," Samael said. "But a real man would have made a baby. You need a son to carry out your legacy. Next time yell out for me and I can have Lilith mix you up a drink so that your cum is more potent."

Ashley didn't want to get up; she was tired. So, after the elders left, I covered her body and left her sleeping in the bed. I quickly washed myself and found a pair of joggers and a t-shirt to wear. As soon as I opened the door, I was shocked to see so many people waiting for me. They were clapping as if I had passed a test or something. I wanted to kick my brother – husband's ass.

"You survived a night with Ashley, now let's go have a couple of drinks," Gethambe stated.

"I can't believe you told everyone that I was a fucking virgin. I told you that shit in confidence."

"Be happy you had her in there screaming out in ecstasy. Because if we didn't hear shit and you came out that door, we really would have talked about you," Rouge said, laughing and patting me on my back.

"I'm well endowed. I knew that I was going to be able to handle her," I said proudly.

"It's not what you have. It's how you use what you have," Stewart said.

"You only say that shit because you have the smallest dick in the pack. Nigga shut up with all that bullshit. Bitches like big dicks," Juice said, smacking Stewart on the back of the head.

"Your momma didn't complain when I rammed all this dick up in her," Stewart laughed, grabbing his dick, trying to prove that he had enough to satisfy his mate.

"Man, fuck what you're talking about," Juice snapped. "I want to know what it feels like sharing your mate with another man?"

Gethambe turned to look at Juice with disappointment filling his gaze. "We've moved past that. I know that it's going to take more than me to keep her satisfied. Now he knows it's going to take more than him. We agreed to keep shit cordial."

"Besides, we have bigger fish to fry. We need to find out where those bitch ass tigers are and rid ourselves of them. We can't stay locked behind these gates forever," I announced.

"True that. We need to discuss that issue over a beer or two. I got a couple of ideas," Rouge stated.

"Is it going to cause a couple of us to sacrifice our life?" Joker wanted to know.

"Nope. Just for Ashely to use her magic to put a locator spell on this," Rouge said, handing me a piece of clothing.

"And what is that?" Gethambe asked.

"A piece of the outfit Lana was wearing the day we got ambushed," he smiled.

~~~~~~~~~~~~~~~~~~~~~

Chapter Twelve

Gethambe

I sat by the waterfall and watched as Ashley and the nannies played with the children. She was so happy here that I didn't want to force her to go back to my home with me. I knew that she would leave if I asked her to, but this place needed her. It needed her more than I did. But as I thought about my home and my way of like, I began to become home sick. I know that it was because of me that things ended up the way that they did, and now I needed to make a choice. Do I stay and spend the rest of my life with a woman I had to share, or do I go home and try to rebuild?

Ashley must have felt that I was deep in thought and became concerned. She made her way over to me and laid on the ground, wrapping my arm around her. "What are you over here thinking about?" she asked.

"Achaemenid," I responded. "I miss home."

"Then go and visit. I will be here with the kids when you return," she replied.

I turned her around to face me before saying, "It's

not a home if I can't have you there with me at my side. Just like the kids are learning the history here, I want them to learn their history of my people and our traditions."

"Then we will go with you."

"Your life is here. These people depend on you. I just want you."

She laughed and said, "I'm not going to leave them forever. We can spend time in your home and then we can spend time here, in Alexandria. You know...alternate back and forth."

"What about Bullet?" I questioned. He had become a big part of both our lives. I had a new type of respect for him and had accepted the fact that my wife loves us both. I didn't want to pull her away from him, just like I wouldn't want him to try and pull her away from me.

"Bullet is a kind and gentle soul. He would understand. I don't think that he would feel any type of way about us leaving for a couple of months. Besides, he is more than welcome to come with us."

That was a thought. But it would leave these people here alone with a king to protect them. And it still bothered me that the Siberian Tigers were still lingering around. They didn't get what they were after and I'm sure they were planning another attack on Alexandria.

"We need a king here, as well as a king in Achaemenid. Although I loved the idea of switching back and forth between the two realms, there needs to be leadership in both places, at all times," I explained. Since the attacks, we have focused most of our time on rebuilding Alexandria and improving the military strategies. I had neglected my people because I knew that they could handle whatever problem that may arise. My people were highly skilled and independent, but I felt that they needed the direction of a king.

"Then, the boys will go to Achaemenid with you and the girls will stay here with Bullet. I will travel between the two places, spending a week at a time with each of my husbands and my children," she suggested. It sounded good, but I didn't want a part time queen. I wanted to spend my entire life waking up to Ashley and had plans on putting more babies into her womb. I know that sounds selfish of me, but she is my reason for breathing.

"I want you every day," I confessed.

She looked at me and felt the love I had for her. And I could feel the love that she has for me, but I could also see that her heart was torn. Her feelings for Bullet have grown and I knew she didn't want to leave him. And I wouldn't ask her to.

Surprisingly she said, "I want you every day too. And I'm willing to leave all this behind me to be with you."

"But what about Bullet? I cannot ask you to give up what you share with him for me. And what about these lands? They thrive because of the power your spirit generates."

"Bullet can come visit us whenever he likes. I can always use the portal to travel between the two realms. I can visit here to ensure the land continues to prosper and live at home and be a caring wife and loving mother to the children. I pledged my life to you and you have always been my first love," she confessed. Everything sounded so good, but I was concerned about Bullet.

Before we could finish our conversation, Rouge

came racing toward us in his beast mode. *"There is a strange man at Ashley's old compound,"* she said telepathically.

"Is he mortal or immortal?" She answered aloud.

"You heard him?" I questioned.

"Of course. I am of wolf descent too. I don't have to flip a switch to hear your voice. I can understand what you are saying as a wolf and what Bullet is saying as a lion. I can also have private conversations with any of you. The only thing I'm having a problem with is understanding those damn Siberian Tigers. They talk in the ancient tongue and their accent is heavy."

I was amazed at how well she was adapting to her powers. "What about Serenity?"

"She is the same way. She can hear everyone. So be careful of your thoughts," she laughed. "Something is different about her. When we are close, her powers dominate mine. She is going to be a powerful and great queen one day. She too is gaining her strength from the temple. I guess because she fed from my breast."

"Look, fuck all of that. There is a strange man at

your old domicile that we need to investigate. The Canine
Crew said that he shows up there every day," Rouge
interrupted.

"Do you think it's one of the Siberian Tigers?" I
questioned.

"I'm not sure. But I think we should go there and
check it out?" Rouge responded.

"Let me gather the kids and we all can travel to
Achaemenid together," Ashley said, getting up and
running over to the nannies.

"You're going to let her go and pull the kids away
from here?" Rouge questioned.

"I miss our home. This place is beautiful and
relaxing, but I miss our way of life," I answered.

"And what about Bullet? How do you think he's
going to take the news of Ashley and the kids moving back
to Achaemenid? She is his wife too," Rouge asked with
great concern.

"We are about to find out. Here he comes," I
replied.

Rouge shifted into his human form and was

immediately covered when Serenity said, "Clothes."

As Bullet approached, it almost broke my heart. His spirit was full of energy and he was happy. He was spending time with the woman he loved and had become attached to all the children. They were just as much a part of his life as they were a part of mine.

"Ashley told me," he said as he approached me.

"And how do you feel about her going home with me?" I wanted to know.

"Her love for you is so much deeper than her love for me. I'm going to have to adjust. She promised to visit with me often, but she will primarily be with you. That is just how it is being a sloppy second," he answered. I could hear the hurt in his voice as he tried to laugh it off. I almost thought that he was holding back his tears.

"Nigga, don't think of yourself as a sloppy second," I told him. "You are a king of a thriving community. I'm sure your father would have been proud of you."

"My father," he whispered. "Son-of-a-bitch! My father!" he yelled.

Ashley came rushing over to us and looked at him concerningly. "No," she said.

"Okay...am I missing something here?" Rouge asked.

"I don't know, because I don't understand what the fuck is going on either," I answered.

"The attack on the city. The elder mountain lion. I believe he is my father. Meet me in the historic library. I need to look something up," Bullet said, morphing into his lion and racing off.

I looked at Rouge who looked at me in confusion. "I thought that nigga's daddy was dead?" Rouge asked.

"They haven't seen him around here in decades. When he switched sides and started fighting for the other team, he was banished from Alexandria," Ashley explained.

"Well I'll be a monkey's uncle. Why didn't he notice him?" I asked.

"I don't know. It could be because he was a young cub the last time he saw his father," Ashley answered.

"Well have the nannies gather the kids and get

them ready for transport. We need to handle two issues now. One, the entity that keeps showing up at your old residence and two, Bullet's demonic father. What in the hell are we in for?"

As Ashley gave orders for the nannies to pack the children's things and get them ready to depart, we all raced to the historic library to find out what it is that Bullet remembered about his father. As we burst through the doors, Bullet was standing at the table with a huge, old book opened. He was running his finger down each line obtaining information about Alexandria. As he finished the section he was reading, he looked terrified.

"Serenity is growing fast and will soon hit puberty," he said.

Ashley grabbed her chest and I could see the tears swell in her eyes. "What is it," she cried out.

Bullet turned the book to me so that I could see the picture of a small golden box. It was decorated with beautiful swirls and ancient wording. I heard of a box like this before but didn't get what he was trying to show me.

"My father showed me this when I was a kid,"

Bullet said.

"So, Serenity will inherit a lot of money?" I asked, looking at the golden box in the picture.

"Shit. We have plenty of that," Rouge laughed.

"No," he answered. His tone was serious. "Serenity is the key to open Pandora's box."

"Man, that shit is only a legend. I believe they said Zeus created Pandora and gave her away to Epimetheus. Along with her came a box that she opened. It was supposed to have unleashed all these bad things into the world and the only thing left was hope," I said, nonchalantly.

Rouge and I laughed because it was told as an old wive's tale to entertain us while we were children.

"Partial truth," Bullet said.

"Meaning what?" I inquired.

"Pandora was the forbidden fruit that caused havoc in this realm. She was a cursed woman made from Lilith's blood by Zeus."

"How did Zeus get my ancestor's blood?" Ashley questioned.

"It was given to Zeus by his brother, Hades…The God of the Underworld."

"Okay…I'm lost," Rouge said. "What in the fuck are you trying to say?"

"I'm trying to say that when Lilith left the Garden of Eden and turned her back on the Almighty, she married a half-breed archangel – demon and was given demon powers. Hades gave Lilith's blood to Zeus to create Pandora."

"Why Lilith's blood?" I questioned.

"Because Lilith was the first succubus created. She was as beautiful as Aphrodite but as cunning as a serpent. She is what Zeus needed to infiltrate Prometheus's home and punish him for stealing fire and giving it to mankind," he answered.

"Why would Zeus be mad at Prometheus for giving mankind fire?" I asked, intrigued by this newfound story that was being told to us.

"Because the humans began to worship Prometheus and not Zeus. This in turn made him jealous but if he killed Prometheus himself, he too would have been sent to the Underworld with his brother."

"So, he sent Pandora to Prometheus as a gift?" Rouge asked.

"No. He knew that Prometheus would suspect something, so he gave her as a gift to his brother, Epimetheus. He was so captivated by her beauty that he married her in secrecy. For a wedding present, he gave them a small golden box and told them not to open it. But Pandora was filled with curiosity and opened it while her husband was sleeping. When she did, it killed the humans that worshiped Prometheus and his family. The only one spared was Pandora."

"So why is Serenity in danger? I have Lilith's blood flowing through me as well," Ashley hissed.

"Because you can not be given to anyone as a gift. You have carried children, but when Serenity reaches puberty, she can be the virgin sacrifice to rid this realm of our existence. Like Pandora, she will survive, but the rest of us will die. Serenity will be the thriving power to keep Alexandria alive and they can use her to conquer other realms," he explained.

"But I'm not giving them my daughter," Ashley huffed.

"And neither will I," I growled.

"But her biological mother can," Bullet revealed.

"Nooooo!" Ashley screamed, collapsing on the floor.

I ran to my wife and picked up her body. As I held her close to me, I looked at Bullet and asked, "How do we keep her safe?"

"By keeping Serenity away from Lana," she answered.

"We can put security with her around the clock. I can double the roving security here and at Achaemenid," Rouge announced.

"We need to use only people we can trust. We need to keep the gates to both realms closed as much as possible. I've noticed that they move in stealth mode like the lionesses. We can go between worlds using the portals," I directed.

"Can't Lana go through the portals?" Bullet inquired.

"Not without an elder or blessed king opening it for her," I explained.

"Do the Siberians have a blessed king?" Rouge asked.

"I'm not sure. In all my years, I have never seen one come through the Portal of Life," I answered.

"Neither have I. But then again, I have never saw a Siberian Tiger leave their native lands," Bullet answered.

"I think we need to get to the temple and call on the elders. We need to know how much they know about them and why they are trying to kill off the wolves and the mountain lions," I said, making my way to the door.

Before I could get down the steps of the historic library, GG came running towards me. My heart dropped into my stomach because I knew she wasn't coming to tell me anything good. The expression on her face said something horrifying had just happened.

"Gethambe...Gethambe! She's gone. I only turned my back for a minute to finish packing her things. When I turned back to her, all I could see was a flash of light. Serenity is gone!" she yelled hysterically.

Bullet and Rouge came running out of the library and I'm sure they heard what she said. I ran with lighting speed as I raced to the temple, still holding my wife in my arms. I busted into our chambers to see that everyone was accounted for except my precious daughter, Serenity.

By this time, I was surrounded by Joker, Stewart, Juice, and Rouge. I walked over to the bed and laid my wife on top of the blanket and turned to my crew and stated, "You know I'm going to kill her?"

"Send me to Edom so I can notify my parents of her wrongdoings," Rouge said.

"Is this going to cause a rift between us?" I needed to know.

"I've told you before, my nigga. She may be family by blood, but I live to serve my king and what she did was foul. She needs to die for all that she has put Serenity through. She is innocent, and my sister is using her for her own personal gain. I'm loyal...you are my family," Rouge answered.

"What about Pax?" Stewart inquired. "We don't want to piss him off."

"He is loyal to my father," I answered. "I will tell him what is going on and he can deal with Pax."

"Are we still going to Achaemenid?" Joker asked.

"I think it's best that Ashley and the kids stay here. I know an old sorceress that is rooted with old magic that can place a protection spell on the temple. She can even block the portal from being used by anyone other than us," Bullet answered.

"Why are you just telling us about her?" I questioned.

"Because with her power comes a price," he answered. "But we will talk about that later. Let's get moving because we don't have much time to work with."

I opened the portal and sent Rouge to Edom to talk with his mother and father about Lana. We made sure that Ashley was comfortable and that she was surrounded by a team of caregivers and nannies for the children. She was beginning to scare me because her necklace was barely glowing, and she was still in a deep sleep.

I advised Juice that once we arrived in Achaemenid, he was to make his way to Ashley's old home and detain the stranger that continues to lurk around her home.

Bullet went after the sorceress while we made our way back to Achaemenid. I wanted to hold a conference and discuss what were our options and what steps we needed to take to protect our people and our way of life.

~~~~~~~~~~~~~~~~~~~~~~~~~

Chapter Thirteen

Lana

"Abrey, do you think that Bullet knows that you are the one behind all of this?" I questioned. He seemed to be a bit more distracted since the beginning of this relationship. I know that he is holding some secrets about his past, but I wasn't quite sure what they were. He made me nervous at times when I caught him staring at me. I felt like he was analyzing my soul.

"He doesn't know anything. He's a smart boy and I have kept my eye on him as he struggled through this life, but I'm sure that he doesn't know that I was the one who slashed his throat," he answered.

"But he still managed to live," Lucas said.

I liked him. His words were harsh but with his soft voice, they flowed so smoothly from his lips. He was shorter than I would have preferred, his skin was cinnamon, and his eyes were this alluring color of sage green. He had my heart the first day he appeared to me in my dream.

It was right after that jackass told me that he was

going to marry Ashley and he wanted me to accept her into our life. Fuck that whorish bitch. Although he told me that I would be considered his first wife, I would still feel like I was his second. He cared nothing for me. Ashley had his heart from the first day he smelled her funky pussy.

"No. He died but that witch beat Anubis to his soul. Then I was told that someone sacrificed their life for his," Abrey stated.

"You should have killed everyone there," he spat.

"If I would have done that, how would we have been able to get into the temple to snatch the girl?"

"That is what we had Lana for. The temple recognized her as a member of their pride. It was nothing for me to teleport her within those walls and teleport her out with the girl. What I needed you to do was find the box."

I was gawking as I listened to him. He was so assertive and calm. Even when he was mad, his voice never became elevated and his demeanor never changed. Lucas was everything I needed in a man. He was the complete opposite of Gethambe; he made everything about me.

"Why do you hate the mountain lions so much? We are practically brothers," Abrey asked him.

"Because they are weak. They allow the love of a god to dictate their strength. They eat when they tell them it's okay to put food in their mouths, they marry who they tell them to marry, and they worship them without getting anything in return. Your people are nothing more than pussycats," he chuckled.

"We were protectors," I could hear the anger in Abrey's voice.

"Protectors for a savage group of dogs," Lucas snapped. Then he looked at me and smiled. "Not you, Precious. You're the only thing that was good there."

God, he melted my heart. "I knew who you were talking about. No offense taken," I smiled at him and placed my hand on top of his.

"As soon as I get the golden box, I can rid you of that hideous mistake you made with *Gethambe,* and together we can rule all the realms. I will show you how a true queen should be treated," he said.

I hated the fact that he had to marry my daughter in order to possess her power, but it was worth it to spend my life with a man who appreciated me for who I was. When he made love to me, he sent my body soaring through the heavens, flying with the angels. Sex with Gethambe was okay, but with Lucas, I can fully enjoy all of him. Instead of pounding inside of me and ripping the skin from my body, he takes things nice and slow, giving me the opportunity to savor the moment.

But it was more than just sex with him. He had a way of making a woman feel like a woman. Lucas opens doors for me, he listens to my ideas and appreciates my input, he puts my needs first, and I love how open and honest he is.

When he first appeared to me in a vision, he told me that it would take him time to love me but if I would help him and give him time, I would be the only woman to hold the keys to his heart. I knew in the beginning that there was nothing between us, but now, things are different.

"I'm going to go check on Serenity," I advised him.

He walked over to my chair and helped me to slide it backwards as I got up from the table. Abrey was even gracious enough to stand up out of respect.

"Please don't hurt the child while you're visiting with her. Only she can open Pandora's box," Abrey said.

"I may not want or like the child, but I am not stupid enough to do something to hurt her. I know how important she is to our cause," I snapped.

"No offense, My Lady," he said.

I gave Lucas a passionate kiss and left the men to discuss business. As I walked through the hallway, I laughed at the female tigers who turned their noses up at me. They felt betrayed by Lucas because he chose me as his mate and not one of them. And the day that I arrived, there was a great fight that broke out within this compound. They were demanding that he return me to my kind and he killed the loudest one and dared anyone else to speak unkindly of me. Since then, none of the females talk to me, unless we are in front of Lucas and they have to answer a question.

We were staying in an old hotel building right

outside of Winslow, not far from my den. Before my arrival, Lucas had the place totally remodeled. Everything here was beautifully decorated and new. My only issue was, they kept this place ice cold. They didn't do well with the heat since we were located in Arizona, they struggled with leaving during the daytime hours. When they had to go out during the day, they had to allow for time for their cars to cool before getting in them.

I took the elevator up to the penthouse suite where I lived. When I stepped off the elevator, I was greeted by the servant girls that were human but knew about our shape shifting abilities. Because Lucas couldn't trust his pride with me, he brought in some help...or should I say kidnapped.

"Where is the girl?" I barked.

"She is in her room, sleeping peacefully," one of the girls answered.

"Has she been awake at all today?"

"No ma'am. Even when I shook her and tried to give her some fresh berries and milk, she did not wake up," she replied.

"Be gone," I told them.

I walked over to the wall of windows and looked out over the land. Although I had officially denounced my people, I missed feeling like I was a part of something. I missed running miles across the desert, hearing the voices of people I knew, and interacting with people like myself. For the most part, I was happy…but I couldn't shake the feeling of being lonely.

I knew that my family had probably disowned me by now. And it broke my heart to wonder what my father thought of me. I thought that maybe if he hadn't babied me as much as he did, I would have turned out a better person. Not to say that he did a god-awful job of being a father because he didn't, he was stern but loving. But I can blame my behaviors on Cherish. She taught me that nothing mattered more than wearing the crown. She used to brag about the power she held while being married to the king's best friend and protector. And when they decided to pair me with Gethambe, her nose flew higher in the air.

But all that is ancient history now. I have made my

decision to be where am I and be with who I wanted to be with. It didn't matter to me now that my mother or father didn't approve of my actions, all I cared about was that I was finally free and living my life without being placed in a small box.

I decided to go and check on Serenity; I hadn't laid my eyes on her sense I snatched her little ugly ass from Bullet and Gethambe. It repulsed me to smell Ashley all over her body. I couldn't give her to Lucas fast enough.

I walked to her room and flung the door open. I saw her body jump so I knew then that she was playing sleep. I walked over to the bed and asked her once, in my nice voice, to get up and bow before her queen. The insubordinate bitch ignored me and continued to play possum.

Rage grew in me like a wildfire. So, I snatched the covers back off her body and grabbed a hand full of her hair and dragged her ass out of the bed. She was yelling and kicking wildly, trying to free herself from my grip. But I had wrapped her long hair around my wrist and drug her into the living room.

The servant girls came running from their quarters and waited for me to let her loose before running to her side. They held her close to their bosoms and cried with her while I laughed.

"You are so ugly," I laughed. "Look at you. You're black with nappy hair just like Ashley. No wonder she loves you," I said, tickled to death by her appearance.

"Why do you hate me?" she cried. "I am your daughter. I came from your womb."

I immediately stopped laughing and perfected my bitch face. "Oh god, please don't remind me," I said to her.

"What did I do to you, Mother?" she questioned.

Hearing her voice pissed me the fuck off. So, just like my father slapped the shit out of my mother, I slapped slob from Serenity's mouth. "Never refer to me as your mother," I warned her. "I hate you with every drop of blood in my body. The gods should have taken you instead of my boys. You are the devil," I told her, as my body started shaking in anger.

I didn't see her as my daughter. She was an

abomination from hell, the seed of Lucifer himself. She didn't look anything like me, she resembled Ashley. Seeing that repulsed me even more.

She had blood spilling from her mouth. When I looked down onto my beautiful white carpet and saw that drops of blood were on it, my anger reached an all new high. As the servant girls scurried about the room to gather cleaning supplies and bandages, I grabbed Serenity by her hair and mushed her face down into her own bloody mess.

"Look at what you did to my carpet!" I yelled.

She cried and yelled out for someone to help her. "God please!" she cried. "Please help me!"

"There is no God here. Just me," I snapped.

As those words escaped my lips, I heard Serenity's voice, but it was deep and demonic. "You will pay for all the pain you have caused me. All I wanted from you was love and all you offered me was pain. Your reign on this world ends tonight."

She stood up and looked at me with cherry red eyes. Her hair was blowing wildly, but there was no wind, and her skin was a black as midnight. I watched as her face shifted; it was a cross between a cat and a wolf. She extended her golden claws and prepared herself for battle.

"As your father once said to me, I'm too much of a cat to be fucked by a pussy," I laughed. I pulled my hair up into a sloppy knot, kicked off my heels, and half shifted into my wolf. "Bring it on bitch."

She came toward me at top speed, her teeth were extended along with her claws. She moved so quickly that I could barely see her. But when my eyes were able to focus, she was already in the air and coming down onto me.

Her fist slammed into my face knocking me down onto the ground, then she yanked me up onto my feet and planted her knee into my side, not once, not twice…but three times. With each impact I could feel a rib crack, making it hard for me to breathe. And with a quick kick to my mid-section, my body flung into the wall.

I became dizzy as I felt the warm sensation of my blood dribble down my face. I was losing a battle that I hadn't even begun to fight. She was quick, strong, and fierce. I realized that I had underestimated Serenity.

She raced toward me and slammed her body into mine, then grabbed me by my arm and flipped me forward over her shoulder. As my body slammed hard onto the floor, she began to power drive blow, after blow into my side. The pain was unbearable, and I could feel my spirit slipping slowly away.

"I gave you every opportunity to treat me like your child," I heard her say. "And you took every opportunity to treat me like the enemy. So, now I have to beat your ass like a common bitch on the street. You will regret the day that you turned your back on me."

She didn't know it, but I already did. I had walked down the path of death and destruction for so long that I couldn't remember what it felt like to do right. As she continued to slash the life from my body, I saw scenes of my life pass before my eyes.

I remembered all the hugs that my father gave me and how proud I made him as I excelled in school. I remember playing in the rain and feeling those soft drops as they hit my face. I remembered the day I was given the news that I was to marry Gethambe and become the queen of our society. I remembered the day we married and him taking my virginity. I thought that we were going to be together forever. And I remembered the day I gave birth to Serenity and prepared my sons' bodies for burial. And I will never forget the woman who stepped into our lives and stole my life from me. I was ready to leave this life of deceit and betrayal. My soul needed to rest, and I knew as long as I walked this earth, it would never find peace.

Serenity stood me up on to my feet and held me by the back of my neck. I heard the elevator door open and I saw a glimpse of Lucas as he rushed in to save me. But he was too late. I felt a sharp pain in my back and then my spirit shifted from my body. As I turned to see what had happened, I saw Serenity hold my body in one hand and my spine in the other. She had reached inside of my human body and ripped my spine out. I knew then that she was a force to be reckoned with.

I didn't stick around to see what would happen to her because I could feel the Almighty calling me home. My spirit traveled quickly through spirals of light, past stars, and around galaxies. I was moving at the speed of light to land in a place of darkness and despair. As I started to walk through the darkness, I heard voices. I heard voices that seemed familiar to me.

"You thought you escaped hell?" she laughed.

"You thought that the Almighty would forgive your sins?" another voice said.

"After all you did, you really think you deserve peace?" a third voice asked.

"But you forgot to ask him for forgiveness and now, you belong to us." That voice I knew all to well. That was the voice of Lilith.

She appeared out of the darkness with a wicked smile on her face. She was accompanied by Na'amah, Agrat bat Mahlat, and Eisheth Zenunim, who looked at me hungrily.

"Welcome home," Lilith said as she snapped her finger. We were transported down to Hell where they were created and resided when they were not with Samael. Although their quarters were beautiful, I was stripped of all my clothing and presented with the outfit that I would wear for all eternity.

I realized then that I would never die, but I would never live. I would never feel loved or see happiness. I will never rest in peace. I had allowed my hatred for my daughter to consume my essence and fill my soul with revulsion. And now I'm going to pay for my sins with my blood, sweat, and tears.

I cannot believe that I had allowed my soul to end up here. I had so much potential.

"You can start with the floors," Na'amah directed, handing me a toothbrush.

"Is this what I use to clean the baseboards?" I inquired.

They all laughed at me as if my question was stupid. "No, dead queen, that is how you are going to mop our floors. And when you're done with that, you can go to the kitchen and the ladies will teach you how to prepare our dinner," Agrat bat Mahlat said.

"And after I finish my duties, where do I sleep?" I questioned.

Again, they all laughed at me. Then Samael shimmered in and answered for them. "You don't sleep here. There is no rest for the wicked. Welcome to Hell."

~~~~~~~~~~~~~~~~~~~~

Chapter Fourteen

Ashley

I jumped up from my long sleep and yelled out for Gethambe. A lioness came running through the door prepared to fight.

"Gethambe. Where is he?" I questioned.

"You have been asleep for days, My Lady. He is out looking for Serenity."

"I know where she is, and I know what is going on. I have to get to him," I said, jumping up from the bed and running toward the portal.

"My Lady, I was told to have you stay here if you woke," she said, bowing her head to me.

"And who's going to stop me from leaving?" I snapped, standing at the entrance to the Portal of Life and holding my necklace in my hand.

"Safe journeys, My Lady. We will continue to care for the kids until you return.

"Thank you," I answered as it opened, and I walked into the bright spiraling light show. As I made my way from Alexandria to Achaemenid, I couldn't shake the vision I had. I needed to get to Gethambe and Bullet and tell them that Serenity had grown into a young woman and that she was okay…at least for now.

As I entered Achaemenid, I ran through the halls until I found a guard. He told me that everyone was in the conference room. I raced to its location and swung the door open. I was out of breath and looked like a mad woman.

"I know where she is!" I shouted.

Everyone turned and looked at me as if they were surprised that I was standing in the doorway.

Gethambe and Bullet both stood, but only Gethambe made his way towards me. He stood in front of me for a moment and then pulled me close to him.

"We thought that you had been cursed. You have been asleep for so long, we didn't think that you would ever wake up," he said. I have always seen Gethambe as a strong man – unbreakable. But today, I saw the love and compassion that he had for me when tears streamed down his face.

"I'm fine," I told him, enjoying the flood of

passionate kisses.

"I love you. With all my heart and soul, Ashley, I love you," he cried.

"And I love you," I answered. "But I need to tell you something,"

Gethambe pulled me into the conference room and pushed me into Bullet's arms because he knew that he was worried about as well. I gave Bullet a hug and kiss and then took my seat at his left side while Bullet sat on Gethambe's right. I swiftly looked over the room to see who was all there and my eyes stopped when I saw Pax.

"Lana is dead," I blurted. "I watched as her spine was pulled from her back. The very person she mistreated was the very person who took her life...Serenity."

He tried to hold himself together, but he couldn't. He broke down in front of everyone. I hated to tell him what I had seen, but he needed to know.

"Do you know where they are?" Rouge questioned, trying to help his father pull himself together.

"Yes. But I have other news about Lana," I said. I knew that what I was about to say was going to blow everyone's mind. "She's not your daughter, Pax."

He looked at me with his eyes filled with hatred. "What did you just say?" Hid tone was hostile, alerting the pack to protect me.

"Cherish lied to you. I saw it. Lana isn't your daughter. She is the daughter of Cherish and Abrey. Bullet, that was your sister," I stated.

Pax's body morphed, and he lunged across the table. He was coming for me and I was prepared to stop him dead in his tracks. "Peace be still," I murmured. Pax's body was hovering in the air over the conference table. He could hear my words, but he could not move his body.

"Let me show you something," I whispered to him. I held out my hand and a hologram popped up. Cherish's life was playing like an old black and white movie.

We watched as she made love to Abrey and made a blood sacrifice to Lucifer to conceal Lana's identity. She too was a wolf and lion hybrid. Cherish needed a daughter so that she could have the life she desired.

"Bullet. This is why they never told you about your mother. You and Lana were from the same litter. Pax didn't know because he wasn't here when Cherish gave birth. You too are a lion and wolf hybrid," I explained as the events continued to play.

"What?" Bullet questioned, falling backwards into his seat. "I don't have wolf traits."

"Lucifer made them submissive in you so that nobody would ever know Cherish's dirty little secret."

When the events that were playing ended, I unfroze Pax's body. He too was stunned by the turn of events in his life.

"Is he my father?" Rouge questioned.

"Yes. You are a true wolf. You are his son and Cherish is your mother," I answered.

"The trickery," Pax spat.

"Summon that witch," Jabari ordered.

With a snap of my finger, Cherish was standing front and center and ready to face her deceptive past.

"Where am I?" she asked confused.

"Mother?" Bullet asked.

She looked at him confused. "What?"

"Come clean already. Ashley has told how you

played bait and switch with me and the kids. Lana wasn't my daughter and Bullet is your son. Is there anything else you want to tell us? Sweetheart."

"Don't believe that rubbish," she said. "She is your daughter."

"Woman, if you continue to lie to your husband I will have your head ripped from your body!" Jabari yelled.

"I was tired of living like a commoner. You couldn't produce a daughter if the gods gave you the recipe. She was our way into Edom. So what I pulled a few strings, you loved her as your own, so therefore she is yours."

I was surprised that she felt no remorse for her actions. She was fine with the deal that she had made with the devil in order to get what she wanted. I knew that Cherish was a selfish person, but no one could have told me that she was this selfish.

"Way to go Mother," Rouge said. "You don't have to worry about her any longer though, because she's dead."

"Well, problem solved," Cherish replied, shrugging her shoulders.

This time, I didn't attempt to stop Pax's attack. He morphed into his wolf, leaped across the table, and ripped her head from her body. But that wasn't enough to satisfy his thirst for her blood. He continued to rip her body apart until it was totally dismembered. After he was finished, he ran out of the room and away from Achaemenid.

The servant girls came into the conference room and began cleaning as we sat there in silence. Nobody knew what to say or who to say it to. Bullet was a hybrid, Cherish was his mother, Lana had been killed by Serenity, and Rouge tried to wrap his mind around the fact that Bullet was actually his half-brother.

"I know where Serenity is, and we need to get to her before Lucas persuades her to open Pandora's box," I whispered.

"Where is she?" Gethambe questioned.

"She is being held on the top floor of that old hotel off of Route Sixty-Six," I answered.

"Who is Lucas?" Jabari asked.

"Lucas is the leader of the Siberian Tigers. They were shunned for not believing in or worshiping the

Almighty. They are inhabitants of Russia but now they are back to claim their land. All of this once belonged to them years ago. Back then the climate was a lot cooler and they were able to maintain their body temperatures. Now, it's hard for them because of the heat. So, the best time to attack them is when the sun is at its highest. They are slower and weaker during that time."

"Why is it so important for them to open Pandora's box and do you know where it's located?" Gethambe asked.

"If Serenity opens the box, her kind will be wiped out. Because Lucas and his people are distant relatives, they will be safe from extinction and will resume their role as the dominant species. He can mate Serenity with the king of other realms and kill off all the royal bloodlines. He would then be king and Serenity his trophy bride. They could make their own race of cats and the wolves and wild dogs would cease to exist."

"Where is Pandora's box?" Jabari questioned.

"In a chamber beneath the temple. Only Lilith or any of her descendants can obtain it."

"Meaning, Serenity could walk right into the temple and take the box?" Rouge asked.

"Yes. She is in the hands of a mad man and we must move quickly," I warned.

"Then we will mount our attack the first thing in the morning," Gethambe growled.

"There's one more thing that you need to know, Bullet."

"Satan is my father?" he tried to joke.

"Your father is here. Abrey is the lion that slashed your throat."

"Go figure. And you're thinking that I should stay away from the fight because you think I'm going to side with a man that left me because of some promised pussy he couldn't have?" Bullet asked.

"In my heart, I know you would never choose Abrey over the love for me or my children. We are your family. And I would never leave you or believe that you will ever leave me," I said, blowing a kiss to him.

"Mon Cheri, you know my heart. But nothing lasts forever."

I felt like Bullet was holding back from me. That statement caught me a little off guard. We were husband and wife, mated to live out our existence until we retired to Edom. But I wasn't going to press him tonight for information. We were all tired and we have learned a lot about our past. We learned that it was filled with secrets and that we were reliving those past events. Because we were all recycled souls, our spirits were making the same mistakes over and over. This is why there was no peace. None of us had made it the eternal resting place. The Almighty kept recycling us in hopes that one of us would break the loop.

As we all parted and made our way to our chambers, I asked for Gethambe to grant me a few minutes alone with Bullet. He was going through a lot and I needed to be that shoulder for him to cry on.

"I understand," he told me. "Spend this night with him. Bullet needs you. Besides, I have to deal with the intruder that Juice detained. He actually caught that chump lurking around your old residence." I gave him a kiss and made my way to the guest chamber where Bullet was

225

preparing for bed.

I walked through the door and locked it behind me. I started to peel off pieces of my clothes, but he showed little interest. Once I was completely nude, I brushed up against him and still didn't receive a response.

"I know you are mad at me for divulging so much information in front of so many people. But you needed to know."

He turned away from me and made his way to the bed. I was still standing at the sink where he had been washing his face. I was stunned that he was giving me the silent treatment.

"So, you're not talking to me?" I smiled, walking over to the bed. "I know how to make you feel better," I joked. I slid in the bed next to him, but he turned his back to me.

I pulled him back towards me and he laid still on his back. When I looked down at his manhood, I could tell that he wanted me, he was just playing hard to get. I was okay with that and took control of the situation.

I leaned over and inserted him into my mouth and

sucked him passionately while I slid my hand up and down his shaft. He was trying to hold back, but he couldn't help himself and began to thrust his hips slowly as he moaned softly. I didn't know why he was playing hard to get, but like Gethambe, the chase turned me on.

"Fuck," he growled. "Suck that dick."

He was giving me a mouthful of him. I was bobbing my head to a moderate beat and sliding my hand to a smooth rhythm. I held him tight, making the vein protrude from underneath his skin. I could taste his sweet nectar as it slowly seeped from him.

He growled and moaned in ecstasy as I pleasured his hardness with my full lips and soft tongue. I took the extra time to come up for air and roll my tongue around his tip. I could tell that he was loving it because I could feel weak shivers wash over him.

Before he was about to explode, I released him from my velvet confinement and allowed him to calm himself. I inadvertently revved my own engines and now I needed to feel him inside of my wetness.

When he caught his breath, I straddled him and slid

down his hardness slowly. His thickness filled me entirely, igniting a small fire inside of me.

"Tell me you love me," I demanded, slowly swirling my hips while he caressed my breasts. "I need to hear you say those words to me."

He struggled to talk but managed to gather enough breath to say, "I will always love you. In this life or the next. I will always love you, Mon Cheri."

I placed my finger on his lips and hushed him. I could sense that he was worried about the battle that we were to face in the morning. "We are not going to worry about the next life. I need you to be happy in this one…with me," I whispered to him as I ground harder onto him.

I sped up the pace and was now riding him hard. I was bouncing and swirling viciously as I fucked him good. I could feel as he began to swell in me, as his hardness thumped like a trotting horse, and his body tightened. He was close, and I was standing on the edge of a cliff ready to fall hard and fast into the euphoric lake of pleasure.

I could feel a tidal wave of elation run rampant

throughout my body. It was warming every drop of blood and making my clit swell as it begged for a sweet and passionate release.

I could feel Bullet's nails as he dug them deep into my skin. My heart was racing and pounding savagely against my chest. I could barely contain my outburst as I yelled at the top of my lungs as my cream shot violently from my body.

"I'm cumming! Fuck Baby! I'm cumming!"

As my cream poured from my body, I could feel his warm nectar erupting into mine. I fell forward onto his chest as his body convulsed as if he was having a seizure. He held me tight, as if he thought he would never be able to hold me again.

I pulled up just a little and began to kiss his fears away. I wiped the sweat from his face and exposed the handsome native man that was hiding behind the beast.

Before we could say anything to each other, Samael shimmered into our chambers with Lilith. She slid her hand between us and felt my stomach. She pulled her hand away but looked at Bullet with sorrow in her eyes.

"Congratulations, Bullet. Your wife is pregnant. You will be a father," she announced.

"Are you allowing us to keep this seed?" I questioned.

"As a present for all that Bullet has done to keep you safe, I grant you this pregnancy."

I cupped my hands on his cheeks and showered him with a million kisses. I was overjoyed that I was going to give him a child. Now my family would be complete.

"Secrecy isn't the best way to live your life," Samael stated. "I had to learn that lesson the hard way." After saying that, he shimmered away with Lilith.

I lifted my body up and looked Bullet in his eyes. "What is it that you're not telling me?" I questioned.

"I knew about Cherish and Lana. I just didn't feel that it was my place to tell Rouge. In a way, I thought that all this would remain a secret. But your dream brought about the truth. How will my people see me now?" he questioned.

"Is that what's been bothering you?" I laughed.

"That is part of what has been on my mind tonight.

I have held a secret about my heritage from the very people who followed me. I outright lied to them."

"It doesn't matter that you have wolf blood. It matters that you were there to lead them into the light when they needed you the most. You are their king. They are not going to love you any less knowing that you share the blood of a wolf," I told him.

"I suppose you're right," he finally smiled. "I wonder what our children are going to look like? You share the blood of a wolf and cat...I share the blood of a wolf and cat; so, what would our children be?"

"Our children are going to be happy and loved by all three of their parents," I smiled.

I lifted my body from Bullet's and snuggled my close into his. I pulled his muscular arm around my waist and fell swiftly to sleep.

~~~~~~~~~~~~~~~~~~~~~

Chapter Fifteen

Gethambe

I knocked on Bullet's chambers door because it was time for us to make our move. I knocked several times but didn't get a response from him or Ashley. Normally I wouldn't intrude on their personal time, but we needed to get moving. So, I cracked opened the door and yelled his name.

"Bullet! We need to get moving, the sun will be up shortly."

I heard some moaning, so I figured he was still knee deep in Ashley. He needed to pull out and get to moving so, I walked in the door. I could see that Ashley was still sleeping but she was in the bed alone.

I tapped her on the shoulder and woke her up. She opened her eyes and smiled at me. No matter how many times I see this woman, I realize that I love her more and more every day.

"Good morning beautiful," I said, kissing her on her forehead.

"Good morning," she answered. "I have news."

I looked at her and laughed. "I don't know if I want to hear any more news from you."

She laughed and then proceeded to tell me that she was with child.

"Lilith visited us last night and blessed us with our child. She did the same favor for Bullet that she did for you," she told me.

I was happy for them, but it pained my heart. I was trying to put another baby in Ashley myself. I figured that all her children would be by me.

"Where is the happy father?" I asked.

She looked around the room and was stunned that he wasn't still in the bed with her. I eased her mind by telling her that he was probably washing up and getting ready for the day. I told her that I would go and find him while she got dressed. I kissed her on the forehead and told her congratulations again.

I left Ashley in her chambers to get dressed while I looked for Bullet. When I was unable to find him on my own, I solicited the help of my Canine Crew. Although we searched every nook and cranny, we could not find Bullet.

When Ashley arrived in the conference room, I know she could feel the thickness in the air. She began to scan the room and to her dismay, Bullet wasn't in attendance.

"Lilith!" she yelled. "Samael!" she screamed. "Where are you?"

Samael shimmered into the conference room alone and tried to avoid eye contact with Ashley. But she walked right up to him and demanded that he tell her where Bullet was.

"This is not my cross to bear. I cannot tell you where he is. His secret is his alone," he said as he shimmered away.

"I can't worry myself with this right now. We need to go get Serenity and end this foolish war."

I know that Ashley's heart was hurting because she couldn't see Bullet's fate or figure out what he was hiding from her. But she did a good job of covering up her pain.

I quickly went over the plan and we all knew what we had to do to break our daughter out of her prison. We all morphed into our beast and ran at top speed to the edge of the Winslow line to where the hotel sat on the old Route Sixty-Six.

Half of the crew flanked the left side of the building while the other side flanked the right side. My father, Jabri and I went straight to the front door and walked right in. On the bottom floor there were regular humans working. They looked at us with skepticism, but we figured it was because we were totally naked from where we shifted back into our human form.

"Excuse me, Mrs.," I started. "We were robbed, and they not only took or money but our clothing as well. Can you help us?"

The ladies all laughed at us but measured me against my father. This must have pissed my wife off because she came in the front doors like Shera. As her hands flung wildly, the doors flew opened. As she sashayed her way into the lobby, she tossed the humans left and right.

"I don't have the time or patience for this bullshit," she snapped, going to the elevator and pressing the button.

We didn't say anything to her, but we did follow

her lead. They had her baby and she was going to retrieve her. On the elevator I heard her cursing to herself. I could hear her call out Bullet's name, but I couldn't make out the rest of the conversation because she was speaking in tongue.

When the elevator doors opened to the penthouse suite, Ashley didn't even look around for the Siberian Tigers, she stepped out of the elevator and commenced to whooping ass. I looked at my father and he looked at me. We shrugged our shoulders and shifted into our beast and joined in the fight.

I was fighting the ones that were running in from the staircase while my father was fighting those who were protecting the kingpin. In the midst of fighting, I caught glimpses of Ashley and a huge male Siberian tiger rolling around the living room. I feared for her safety but couldn't catch a break from the ones that were coming up from the lower floors.

The fight evened out when Rouge and the rest of my crew arrived. The penthouse was filled with sharp teeth and long claws. You could hear the louds howls and the deep roars as we fought till the death. I was ripping these beasts apart, tearing the skin from their bodies. But they were inflicting just as much pain on me.

I had gashes on my body that were spilling blood like a steadily running faucet. But even with the wounds that I had sustained, I continued to fight violently to save my daughter's life.

When I was able to catch a break, I looked over at Ashley who was pulverizing the large tiger. She was throwing spells, switching between her cat and her wolf, she was tossing him around the room like a rag doll until we all heard a loud voice yell, "CEASE."

We were all paralyzed. The only movement in the room was from Ashley and a much older, Serenity.

"I have grown weary of the fighting. It stops today. I cannot be forced or persuaded to open Pandora's box. So, go home Lucas and take your pride with you. And if I see you in my next life, even than it would be too soon."

Serenity snapped her fingers and our bodies were freed. She looked around the room and then back to Lucas. "You have exactly twenty-four hours to leave this land or

I will rip your spine from your back as I did my mother."

If he didn't realize her strength, he did now. He bowed his head and limped away from her presence with his crew close behind him. As we all began to shift into our human form, she spoke again, "Clothes," and we were all fully dressed.

She looked at her mother and told her that we needed to get to Alexandria so that she could say her final good-byes.

"Good-bye to who?" I heard Ashley ask.

Serenity didn't answer but waved her hand and teleported all of us to Alexandria. As we stood at the gates, we noticed a crowd gathering at the temple. Ashley immediately raced to it, pushing people out of her way. I ran behind her because I knew this couldn't be good.

When she reached the steps, there lie Bullet's body. She walked slowly up to him with tears falling from her eyes.

"We can beat this," she said to him.

"Not this time, Mon Cheri. I gave my life to protect our children's," he said.

"When?" she asked sniffling.

"When I asked the witch to place a spell on the portal. Her price to protect my family was my life."

"You should have waited," she cried. "We could have found a way."

"Don't cry my love. I will see you again," he said with his last breath.

We heard the loud drums of Anubis as he came to collect Bullet's soul. As the spiral swirled opened the ground, Anubis appeared. He extended his hand and we saw as Bullet's spirit rose from his body.

"Can we offer another life for his?" Ashley cried.

"A deal was signed in blood. A favor for the protection of his family. This is a debt that can only be paid for by him," Anubis answered.

Serenity stepped forward and cupped her hands together in front of her.

"Precious jewels," she spoke.

Her hands were instantly filled with the clearest diamonds in the world. She gave them to Anubis and begged that he walk with Bullet to the gates of Heaven.

"No need for gifts, he is guaranteed a generous life in the eternity realm. Then he descended into the ground with Bullet's spirit.

Serenity and Ashley had the body brought into the temple and the priest prepared his body for the ceremony. Once he was dressed in his royal attire, the Canine Crew carried his body to the Nile.

They placed his body on the royal ship that I had built for him. With tears in their eyes, Serenity and Ashley kissed him one last time as the Canine Crew gave the ship a gentle push. As it started to float away, we recited the Serenity Prayer;

God grant me the Serenity to accept the things that I cannot change;

The courage to change the things that I can;

And the wisdom to know the difference between the two.

Living one day at a time; enjoying one moment at a time,

Accepting hardships as the pathway to peace;

Taking, as He did, this sinful world as it is,

Not as I would have it;

Trusting that he will make all things right,

If I surrender to his will;

That I may be reasonably happy in this life;

And supremely happy with Him,

Forever in the next.

AMEN

As we finished the prayer, the archer aimed his bow high toward the sun and shot his arrow. It flew like an angel and landed on its destination. As the sun began to nestle itself behind the snowcapped mountains, the ship burst into flames.

It was then that it began to thunderstorm.

Serenity stood strong, but Ashley fell to her knees in the water. Following suit, both tribes took a knee and bowed their last bow to a great king.

"A part of him will always be with us," I whispered. "We will love his children and talk to them daily about the great deeds their father did for his people."

"It's not fair," she cried. "It's just not fair."

I didn't try to move her. I allowed her to sit there

in the water until she could no longer see his ship. Nobody stood before Ashley, not even the children of the pack or pride.

Today, I lost a good friend, my children lost their father, and my wife lost her second husband.

Although this fight is over, the war has just begun. I made a vow to myself that I was going to revenge my friend's death by killing the Mad King Abrey and finishing that battle with the Siberian Tigers.

Like a wise man once said, "I'm living to fight another day."

To Be Continued

Message to the Reader

First, I would like to thank God for giving me the gift to write these stories. Without my faith in him, I would not flourish as an author or a person.

Secondly, I want to thank my husband and my family for their continued support because without their time, patience, and understanding – I wouldn't be able to give you my best. So, to the man that I love with all my heart...Terence Derone Smith, I appreciate all that you do. Your generosity has not gone unnoticed.

Thirdly, I want to thank Quiana Nicole for taking a chance on me and showing me my potential.

Finally, I thank you...the readers! As a new author, I appreciate your willingness to ride with me on this journey. You guys are just simply amazing!

I hope you enjoy this book as much as I enjoyed writing it. Please leave a review and tell me what you think and keep your eyes open for "Skinwalkers ~ 3", because it's coming soon to Amazon!

Keeping Up With Monica

www.eroticauthormlsmith@gmail.com

www.eroticauthormlsmith.com

https://twitter.com/AuthorMLSmith73

https://www.instagram.com/terrylynsmith/

https://www.facebook.com/authormonicasmith

https://www.facebook.com/terrylynsmith

Psst…Join my secret reading group

www.facebook.com/groups/eroticevenings

21+ Adults Only

Be sure to <u>LIKE</u> our Major Key

Publishing page on Facebook!

CPSIA information can be obtained
at www.ICGtesting.com
Printed in the USA
LVHW041759010419
612563LV00003B/339

9 781798 964330